SUMMER OF

NO REGRETS

SUMMER OF
NO REGRETS

KATE MALLINDER

Firefly

First published in 2019
by Firefly Press
25 Gabalfa Road, Llandaff North, Cardiff, CF14 2JJ
www.fireflypress.co.uk

A CIP catalogue record of this book is available from
the British Library.

ISBN 9781910080948
ebook ISBN 9781910080955

*This book has been published with the support of
The Books Council of Wales.*

Chapter heading images from shutterstock.co.uk

Typeset by Elaine Sharples

Printed and bound by 4edge Limited

To Sophie, Rory, Noah and Tilda
for inspiring me every day
And Mark, for your unwavering support

CHAPTER 1
HETAL

Sasha was filling us in on her post-exam snog. 'It was right after the last maths paper – and you know how stressed that exam made me.'

We all nodded. I remembered the stress: late-night calls, tears and a recurring theme of 'I hate numbers and numbers hate me', which if I'm honest, I struggle to comprehend. Numbers are wonderful. You know where you stand with numbers. Here's why:

1. They follow the rules. A two doesn't suddenly think it'll try being a three. They know their place.
2. They react the same way every time and once you've got the right answer, it'll always be right.
3. You don't have to write opinion pieces in maths. You just have to show the working out.
4. There are no grey areas…

'You still with us, Hetal?' Sasha interrupted my thoughts.

'What?' I said. 'Oh sorry, got side-tracked by ... something.' Despite them being my best friends in the whole world, it's still not a great idea to confess to daydreaming a number love-list. But if I *were* to list my favourite numbers, they'd be 49, 512, 3.14159...

'Well,' Sasha continued, rolling her eyes, 'as we were walking out of the sports hall, he caught my eye. He's not in my maths set, so who knows what his name is.'

'But you know now, right?' said Nell, her eyes wide.

'Sure.' Sasha flicked her hair. 'Let's call him ... Fit Boy.'

Cam sniggered. 'I can't believe you, Sasha. So you got with him right on the sports-hall steps?'

Sasha looked momentarily self-conscious before grinning.

'YOU DID!' shrieked Cam. 'Argh, I was only kidding, but you did.'

'It was the adrenaline rush,' said Sasha, shrugging her shoulders. 'What can I say? Everyone else was hugging, I decided I'd prefer something else, that's all. Perfect end to any maths exam.'

Cam was laughing so hard, tears rolled down her cheeks. 'I can't believe you! That's outrageous!'

Nell was looking shocked but kind of in awe of Sasha.

'So,' I said. 'Was "Fit Boy" any good?'

'He had just the right mix of lips, tongue and teeth,' grinned Sasha.

My brain fired up. What, like a ratio, did she mean?

'Plenty of the first two and none of the last,' she elaborated.

Aha. So a ratio of 1:1:0. Good to know.

Sleepovers don't change much really. We're pretty much doing the same things at sixteen that we were at thirteen except we talk about boys *way* more, the movies are rated higher and my parents have given up telling us to keep the noise down. But other than that, the basics are still the same. It's still me, Cam, Sasha and Nell, all squashed into my bedroom with a mountain of duvets and piles of make-up, all talking at once, laughing loud enough to scare the cat and sharing secrets.

'Are you going to see him over the summer then?' asked Nell, still looking star-struck.

Sasha faltered for a moment. 'I'm not sure.'

'Why not?' I asked. If he had the perfect kiss ratio, and was cute, then why wouldn't she?

'My dad's got a contract in Geneva and he's asked if I want to go and spend a few weeks over there with him.'

What?

'Thought you'd just *casually* drop *Geneva* into the conversation? What the...? Are you going?' asked Cam. Her pale cheeks had flared red, like they always did when she got excited.

'It would be good for my French if I did, and I've never been abroad, so that would be, well, awesome.'

Sasha's face didn't match what she was saying. If it was such a great idea, why didn't she look like she believed it?

'But do you want to go?' I asked.

Sasha ran her hands through her long, wavy hair, pulling it back from her face. 'I don't know. I mean, yes, of course, it's Switzerland! Who wouldn't? But...' She paused. 'But it means leaving Mum. And I don't get to see you guys for ages and this was supposed to be our summer. The summer of us.'

I totally got her. I wouldn't want to go either. Why go somewhere new where anything could happen? Besides, we'd been making plans for this summer for months. I'd made a list (not that this is unusual – I make lists about pretty much everything. Once, I had so many lists on the go, I had to make a list of lists).

After the exams, we would:

- Have massive ice-cream sundaes for breakfast
- Go surfing
- Shop till we dropped in Plymouth
- Camp out
- Go out on Cam's dad's boat
- Watch all the *Harry Potter* movies in a day (& night)

Sasha looked glum, and let her hair fall to one side, covering her face.

'Tough call,' said Cam finally.

Someone tapped gently on my bedroom door and Nani poked her head round.

'I thought I'd say goodnight before I turn in,' she said. Nani lives with us and is, by far and away, my favourite adult.

'Night, Nani.' I looked at her face. Her eyes didn't seem as sparkly as usual and her eyeliner had smudged.

'Night, Mrs M,' said the others.

'Hetal, honey,' said Nani, 'would you help me send an email tomorrow?'

'Sure, no problem. Who are you emailing?'

'My dear friend Elsie. Seems we need to embrace technology. We don't have time to waste waiting for letters to and from Australia.'

There was something different about Nani's face.

Something definitely wasn't right.

'Are you OK?' I asked.

'What me? I'm fine. When you get to my age, it's to be expected.'

We all sat watching my nani from under our duvets.

'The other thing with being my age is that you look back at your life and you can see so clearly where you went wrong. Forgive me, Sasha, for eavesdropping, but I heard you mention a trip abroad and I have some advice. For each of you.'

We were all concentrating on Nani properly now.

'Live your life. Grab it. Seize opportunities when they come along, otherwise you'll end up old women with hearts full of regrets.'

Her voice cracked a little. My usually so jolly, so positive Nani was on the verge of losing it. I looked round at my friends to see if they had noticed too. Sasha was frowning and Nell looked a little terrified. Cam was nodding.

'Nani?' I said softly. 'What's wrong?'

Nani sniffed and wiped her eyes with a tissue. 'I got some bad news today, that's all.'

My heart clenched. What if Nani was seriously ill? What if she had life regrets because she was running out of life?

Nani glanced at me, like she could read my mind. 'I'm fine. Fit and healthy as the next seventy-one-year-old. I'm only telling you this so you don't make the same mistakes.'

I relaxed a bit. So what was it? What had made my lovely, gorgeous inside-and-out Nani so sad?

Nani stepped further into the room, adjusting her dressing gown. 'I'm not going to spoil your sleepover with my troubles. But girls, take it from me, don't put off living: have adventures, do things that scare you. Don't say, I'll do it when I'm older, when I've got a job, when I've got a boyfriend, after I've had kids, when I've retired. Do it now. Spend your time with the people you care about, but don't let them tie you down. You get one chance. Take it. Grab it and don't let go.'

Sasha and Cam were nodding and Nell still looked nervous, as if Nani might make her do something that scared her right there and then.

'You're good girls, you are,' said Nani, looking at

each of us in turn. 'Now I'm going to let you get on with your sleepover.'

'Thanks, Mrs M,' said Sasha. 'Hope we don't keep you awake.'

'Make as much noise as you like,' smiled Nani. 'It's what earplugs were invented for.'

We all laughed.

She blew us a kiss and pulled the door closed behind her.

'Oh, she's dropped something.' Nell picked up a folded piece of paper.

'Give it here,' I said.

'Are you going to read it?' said Sasha.

'No! Of course not.'

'Don't you want to know what it says?' asked Cam.

'Yes, but it's not right.'

'OK, I'll read it.' Cam plucked it from Nell's fingers.

'No,' I cried. 'Don't.' I should have stopped her. I definitely should have stopped her.

'It says it's from Elsie.'

'That's who she wants to email, her friend in Australia,' I nodded. 'They've been friends since forever. Nani said Elsie was her only friend when she first came from India. Then Elsie married an

Australian and emigrated. Not sure Nani's seen her since.'

'And they've kept in touch all this time?' said Nell.

I shrugged. 'They're best mates.'

Cam was busy reading. 'Her handwriting's illegible. If I was your nani I would have suggested emailing ages ago, just so I could know what she's on about.'

'What's it say?' Sasha leaned over Cam's shoulder.

'Hang on. Elsie isn't very well.' Cam's voice softened. 'She's got cancer. The doctors say it's terminal. She's not got long.'

We all went quiet.

'Poor Nani,' I muttered. 'No wonder she's upset.'

I glanced round at my friends, Cam holding the paper, Sasha leaning on her shoulder and Nell looking at me, her brown eyes glistening. They'd known my nani forever, she was always giving us bits of advice.

'Your nani's right, you know,' Cam sighed.

'About what?' said Sasha.

'About living our lives. Seizing the day.' Cam stood up. 'So, how about it? A summer of living life to the max. Full tilt. Who's in?'

'Sounds exhausting,' I said. 'You don't have to be

doing everything, all at once. What if your ideal summer is having a monster lie-in every day?'

We all laughed.

'OK,' said Sasha, 'what about this? A summer of going outside our comfort zones?'

'But my bed is the absolute definition of my comfort zone,' I retorted. 'And I'll never regret a single millisecond I spend in it.'

'That's it!' Cam declared.

'What's it?' said Nell.

'That's what we'll have: a summer of no regrets.'

CHAPTER 2
CAM

I knew exactly where I was going to start. With something that I'd been bugging my foster-mum Jackie about for ages. Last year she stopped me, saying she had right of veto because the legal age was sixteen. But now I'm sixteen, she can go whistle. I set off into town, the morning sunshine already bright. Pulling my sunglasses on I grinned to myself; today was going to be a Very Good Day.

Several hours later, the hairdresser held up the mirror behind me.

'What do you think?'

'But … but it's *pink*!' I said, widening my eyes.

The hairdresser's face fell. 'You asked for Candy Dust, though,' she stuttered.

'Only messing with you. It's great. Cheers.' I mussed up my short and now shockingly pink hair and grabbed my phone. Pink hair and no regrets – I was off to a bitching good start. I snapped a selfie and shared it with the girls: #NoRegrets.

Sasha: *What the hell, Cam? You are ROCKING that look!*
Hetal: *Loving it!*
Nell: *Of all the things to do, it had to be pink hair?!*
Me: *So what about you lot? It's been 3 days. Anyone else done anything yet?*
Sasha: *Want to meet up? I've got some news.*
Hetal: *Good, I hope.*
Me: *The quay?*
Nell: *See you in 5.*

I walked down the hill from the town and across the market square. We always meet up at the second to last bench on the promenade that runs the length of the quay. It overlooks a narrow waterway, which has a pontoon running along the centre, with dozens of little boats moored up alongside it. The air's full of seagulls cawing and the *chink chink* of taut lines against masts. The market was on and stalls selling children's wetsuits, carved wooden mice and secondhand books jostled for attention. I love it here. I love the sea and the way that life by the sea revolves around tide times and full moons.

I was the first at our bench, so I sat munching on a pasty I'd got from the butcher's next to the hairdresser's. A huddle of kids were crabbing on the jetty, squealing whenever one escaped and ran towards them on pointy legs, claws held up. A tern and her chicks were swimming past me, and a man was rowing towards his boat. I love that the people round here never seem to be rushing.

'There she is!' I heard. 'The candyfloss herself.'

Walking towards me was Hetal, never knowingly overdressed in her standard jeans and a jumper, with geeky black glasses. I'm allowed to call her geeky – she totally sees it as a compliment. Next to her, but a pace behind, was Nell, with her usual long sleeves, and then Sasha, who was showcasing her early season tan in tiny shorts, a tied top and sunglasses pushed into her hair and was, of course, the one shouting.

How I managed to deserve friends like these, I will never know.

'Oh, shut up,' I yelled back, which earned a tut from some passing old guy. I resisted the urge to reply with two fingers.

'You look totally freakin' awesome,' said Sasha. 'Honestly. I'm blown away.'

'Thanks.' I grinned. I felt totally freakin' awesome, to be honest.

'Give us some,' said Nell. 'I'm starving.' She took a massive bite out of my pasty.

I gave her what was left. 'So, you said you had some news?' We all looked at Sasha, who beamed.

'I've made a decision about Geneva. I'm going.'

I squealed. 'Brilliant – what made you change your mind? Ah, I'm so jealous! You're swanning off to Switzerland and I'm staring down the barrel of a summer spent working the till in Papa John's hardware shop.'

'It was what your nani was saying, Hetal, the other night. I thought, I need to try it. If I hate it, I can always come home early, can't I?'

'What are you going to do while you're there?' said Nell.

'I don't know. Dad'll be working a lot of the time, I guess, so I get to explore the city, check out the local sights.'

'Check out the local lads, more like,' said Hetal, grinning.

'That thought *had* crossed my mind.'

We sat along the bench, all silent for a moment,

Nell finishing off my pasty. It was going to be weird without Sasha.

'When do you go?' I asked.

'Tomorrow.'

'What?' said Nell. 'Tomorrow? Flippin' heck, you don't hang about.'

'Sorry.' For a split second, Sasha didn't look so happy.

'You sure you're alright about it, Sash?' I asked. There was something bothering her but I couldn't tell what it was. And I bet she wouldn't tell us. That's Sasha all over. Keep it all in and try and fix it herself.

'Yeah. Totally.' Her face was back to normal again, and I wondered if I'd imagined it. 'Sorry about the short notice though. How about we do something today? You know, before I go.'

'Cam, what about your dad's boat?' asked Hetal.

'He's not my dad,' I snapped.

'Right, sorry. But what about the boat? Do you think we could use it?'

Hetal looked all fidgety cos I'd snapped. But I wasn't sorry – it was important. He was a foster-dad, not my real dad. Papa John and Jackie wouldn't stick around once the social money stopped coming. Not like blood, which is forever.

'I'll go and ask him.'

I ran back along the quay, through the market and up the street to the hardware shop. The door jangled as I pushed it open.

'Papa John,' I said, out of puff. 'Can we borrow the boat?'

There weren't any customers in but despite that he didn't answer me. He just gawped.

'Hello?' I said, waving my hands in front of his face. He'd finally lost it.

'Sorry, love,' he said. 'Momentarily shocked into silence by your, um, your hair.'

I'd completely forgotten.

'So? What about the boat?'

It was like I'd not said anything. 'Very … nice,' he went on, looking at my hair from different angles. 'Guess they don't call it shocking pink for nothing.'

'Excuse me?' I said, bristling.

'It's smashing, Cam. Don't mind me. I'm just old-fashioned in my choice of hair colour, that's all. So, what do you want to do with the boat?'

Three years ago, a month after he bought the hardware shop, Papa John had bought a boat. Jackie had argued that they didn't have the money, what with the new business, but he had bought it anyway.

Since then, most weekends he'd taken me out and taught me how to sail, how to moor up safely, the rules of the estuary and countless little tips on how to control it.

'Sasha is off to Geneva tomorrow...'

Papa John's eyebrows shot up.

'Long story. But anyways, we want to do something fun all together today, so could we borrow it? Please.'

I dug deep and pulled the puppy eyes on him. Despite the handicap of my pink hair, he caved.

'Alright then, but be safe. Remember everything I've told you. And no messing about. It's a serious responsibility skippering a boat. Don't let me down.'

I crossed my heart and hoped to die. Not literally – who hopes to die? Then I texted the others. This day was turning out to be the boss.

Half an hour later, with plenty of snacks, swim stuff and suncream, we walked along the jetty until we'd reached *The Sundance Kid*. They'd all been on it before, so they knew how it worked. I started the outboard and manoeuvered the dayboat away from the moored boats, before setting our sights out along the estuary towards Salcombe.

We were lucky that high tide had fallen in the

early afternoon. A few hours different, and *The Sundance Kid* would have been beached and going nowhere.

Following the estuary out, we passed the mouths of small inlets, tucked along the shoreline. Houses with shutters and little boats tied to private moorings lined the water's edge.

'Wow, it's hot,' said Nell, her face flushed. She pulled her hoodie over her head, showing off a polka-dot vest top underneath, the colours bright against her dark skin. 'That's better,' she grinned, and took the suncream Sasha was offering.

Nell never wears short sleeves except when it's just us. I think it's because of her accident, but I can't really remember whether she wore short sleeves before that, so I can't be sure. One thing I know though. She's seriously tough. I mean, if I'd lost half an arm in a boating accident, *everyone* would know about it. And I would have taken it all out on that idiot boat skipper who wasn't wearing the kill cord and who definitely should have received more than a stupid caution. Nell had been swimming and, when the skipper of the boat fell in, the boat kept going. Ploughed right into Nell before hitting the rocks. She was lucky to be alive. But I've never heard Nell complain. Not once. And that's hard core.

'I can't wait to be in that water.' Sasha looked warm too and was gazing out across the water. It made me want to dive in right there.

We raised the sail, and I helmed. The little boat glided along, the breeze brisker than in the harbour. The sun shone down, the light bouncing off the water like it was a million mirror fragments. When we'd got to our spot, Hetal lowered the sail and I secured the anchor, feeling it take on the soft sandy riverbed.

We changed into our swim stuff and dived off the boat. I swam down and down, as far as I could, until my lungs felt like they were going to burst. I touched the bottom then pushed back up to the surface, the sun seeming extra bright after the dark silty water of the estuary. Some people don't like the feeling of deep water; they say it's like the opposite of being up high, but I love it. It gives me a feeling of absolute and total freedom.

'I've got some news too,' said Hetal, as we sat around the boat on the bench seats, drip-drying and munching on crusty fresh bread.

'Really?' Nell looked startled. 'Don't say you're leaving too.'

Hetal chewed her lip. 'It's only for a couple of weeks.'

'What?' I said. 'Where are you going?'

'Well, I wasn't going to. It's only Wales. And it's not tomorrow like Sasha's trip.'

'*What's* for a couple of weeks?' I asked.

'Science camp,' Hetal said.

'Science camp? You're kidding me,' said Sasha. 'I thought they only have stuff like that in America.'

'No.' Hetal looked embarrassed. 'It's quite an honour, actually. It's invite only. You have to be pretty good to get asked.'

'Pretty good?' I asked.

Hetal grinned. 'You have to be in the top one per cent of science grades in the country.'

'Hm, so above average then,' said Nell. 'Well, congratulations – that's such an achievement. Why weren't you going to go?'

'I didn't want to be away from home. And you guys, obviously.'

'But miss out on science camp?' Sasha was struggling to keep her voice straight.

Hetal laughed. 'You might not fancy it but, honestly, if it was here in Devon it'd be my dream holiday. They've got some really cool experiments planned, they have scientists coming in to talk about their research and there's tons of ace stuff going on. The lodges are all named after famous scientists and the teams are elements from the periodic table.'

'Nice one, Hetal. That sounds like ... just your thing.'

Hetal smiled. 'I am a bit nervous, though. I've never been away from home before. I missed the French trip cos I had that bug, remember?'

I tried not to but couldn't help catching Sasha's eye. Hetal noticed the glance that passed between us.

'Did you know I didn't really have a bug? Why didn't you say anything? Now I feel stupid. But I just couldn't face going. And I feel the same about science camp. What if I hate it? I don't know anyone there. What if the food is awful? What if there's something even worse that I haven't even thought about? These are only the things I can *imagine*.'

'You'll be great.' Nell gave her a hug. 'Better than great.'

'You've got to give it a go, Hetal,' said Sasha, towelling her hair. 'You never know, it might be *better* than you expect.'

Hetal grinned at Sasha. 'No regrets, huh?'

Sasha nodded, smiling back.

'OK,' I said. 'So, you're off to Switzerland, Sasha,

and Hetal, you're disappearing to deepest, darkest Wales. Nell? Have you got any plans you haven't told me about? Not popping over to Australia this summer?'

'Are you kidding?' said Nell. 'As if my mum would let me out of her sight.' Nell's mum is an uber-control freak.

'But she lets you come out on the boat with us,' Hetal pointed out.

Nell raised an eyebrow. 'Who says she knows.'

CHAPTER 3
SASHA

The heat engulfed me as I stepped onto the metal steps leading off the plane. Excitement fizzed as I looked out over the shimmering tarmac. I straightened my top, pulled my sunglasses down over my eyes and ran a hand through my hair. Watch out Geneva, Sasha Wilson has arrived.

Geneva's airport was busy with people and planes and fuel trucks, but I could see the mountains rising above all that, grand and impressive even at this distance. I breathed in the air, thick with aviation fumes.

Mum had put on her brave face when I left. Told me to have a great time. That it would be good for me to spend some quality time with my dad. That she had loads of plans for while I was away and I wasn't to worry about her. Even so, the brave face never lies.

But I was here and she was there, so I put Mum out of my mind and went along with the crowd, collected my suitcase from the baggage carousel and walked through the airport to the arrivals lounge. Everywhere stunningly dressed women strolled with a casual chic, appearing completely unruffled by the searing temperatures. Tanned men in cream suits and open-necked shirts clutched leather attaché cases and immaculately folded newspapers. My shorts and T-shirt, which had felt perfect in Devon, were out of place here. And how did they do it? I felt a hot, melting mess compared to everyone else and I was wearing a fraction of the clothes. Every time the doors opened, new waves of hot air rolled towards me. But who cared? I was here on holiday, not to win some 'who can wear the most clothes and still look totally chill' award.

I searched all around me. Dad had said he would meet me here but I couldn't see him anywhere. A fit boy leaning against the wall caught my eye. He smiled. I held his gaze. No harm in looking.

'Natasha, over here.' It was Dad, looking a little greyer than when I'd last seen him. When was that?

A year ago, at least. I noticed he was in the smartly-dressed, suit-wearing chic crowd. And I was in Devon's finest flip-flops.

'*Ma belle fille*,' he said when he got to me. I went to hug him as he leaned to kiss me on the cheek. Totes awkward. Behind Dad I could see the boy grinning.

'Which way is the car?' I asked, wanting to move this cringe-fest out of public view. Well, out of that boy's view. But Dad wasn't listening.

'It has been too long. Let me look at you. I think you have grown, *n'est-ce pas?*'

'I guess so. It's good to see you too.' The words 'let's get out of here' were on the tip of my tongue but I couldn't make myself say it. I would have with Mum. But Dad? It was different somehow.

Finally, he picked up my suitcase and linked his arm into mine, which felt odd. I'd not seen him in ages and then he's all father/daughter intense? I'd never really noticed it before he'd left, but Dad was way more huggy and kissy than Mum. Perhaps that was a French thing, or maybe that was just him. Either way, it felt like we were all out of step, like there was music playing but neither of us could find the beat.

'So, *ma petite*, tell me all your news. How were

the exams? And how are your friends? And your mother?'

Huh. Where to start with filling my dad in on a year of my life. 'There's no rush, Dad. We've got ages to catch up.'

He squeezed my arm. 'This is true, but I want to hear about it all. I feel I don't know this young woman before me.'

Which I guess he didn't. I was a kid of ten when he left and, apart from a handful of short and infrequent visits, I'd not really seen much of him since. How could he know who I was now?

'So,' he said with a flourish, opening the door to the apartment, 'this is our humble abode for the summer.'

I walked into the open-plan kitchen-come-sitting area. Shutters across the windows threw stripes of light across the dark room. Dad moved to put on the air conditioning, setting off a soft hum and a cool breeze. He opened the balcony windows and pushed back the shutters, letting sunlight flood in. Out of the window I could see roofs, stepping down to the lake. Lake Geneva. A vast, glittering blue stretching out into the distance with mountains towering above the opposite shore.

'What do you think?'

'It's … it's beautiful.'

Dad grinned. 'I'll put your case in your room.'

I pushed the windows wider and stepped out onto the balcony. A couple of chairs stood to one side, the metal burning hot when I tried to sit down. I leaned on the wooden balcony instead and looked and looked. It felt like my eyes were superglued to the view.

I texted the others.

Me: *Arrived OK. Staying in a village just outside of Geneva. Freaking gorgeous! #NoRegrets*

I attached a photo and sent it.

The streets below the apartment were nearly empty. They shimmered in the heat. A moped buzzed past. I daydreamed about maybe a local boy, with a moped, with room for an extra on the back. In the distance a dog barked. The air was warm and smelled of fresh coffee and a flower of some kind. I sighed. Perhaps this was going to be a good holiday after all.

The sun was so hot, I could feel my skin burning, so I walked back into the coolness of the apartment to find my suncream. As I rummaged through my bag, I could hear Dad on the phone, talking in rapid French.

Dad had said this holiday would be brilliant for my French, especially as I was planning to study it next year, so I tuned my ear in and listened. I couldn't catch every word. He was talking to someone called Clarisse. Perhaps someone he works with. He was speaking really quickly, but he seemed to be saying she couldn't arrive yet. It was too soon. He needed more time. Time to explain. She must be someone on the same contract as Dad. Perhaps she's not needed yet.

Then I heard my name. And although my French isn't perfect, I was pretty sure he said, 'Stop worrying. Once you arrive I'm sure Natasha will love you.'

For someone who'd not seen me for a year, he seemed pretty damn sure that I was going to love whoever the hell this Clarisse was.

That evening we went out for dinner to a restaurant on the lakeside. The temperature had dipped as the sun set, and the village buzzed as the locals came out to socialise. The breeze was full of the chatter of the diners, the quiet lapping of the water against the wall and the loud chirping of crickets. Dad had gone to order drinks from the bar and I sat looking out over the lake. The air felt as if it was made of something different here, like there was excitement and possibility mixed into it. Despite having travelled all day, my body itched to explore the lake, walk along the bank, breathe in the air.

'*Bonsoir, mademoiselle.*' I turned to find the most beautiful person I had ever seen. Literally. No. Exaggeration. Olive skin, dark eyes and black hair that would have fallen in his eyes if he hadn't pushed it back. You know how you get winded if you fall funny on a trampoline and all the air gets knocked from your lungs? Well, that. Totally.

I must have been gasping for air, because he brought me a glass of iced water. He left it on the table and smiled. Which, honestly, if he was trying to help me get my breath back was not working. Another table called for the bill, and he went to serve them, leaving me gripping the table legs under the tablecloth and wondering why my body and mind had let me down so completely when it was clearly crucial I pulled off the charming and sophisticated thing.

Over dessert Dad quizzed me about exams. There was no more sign of the waiter. I kept my eyes fixed on the candle in the centre of the table, picking away the dried drips of wax that had rolled down the edges on previous evenings and had got stuck to the wickerwork candle holder. I answered all the questions, but couldn't get Clarisse out of my head. Who was she? Why would I be meeting her? And why would I love her? I tried to tell myself it could be something really innocent – it could be a housekeeper, someone to keep an eye on me while Dad was at work. But my brain's not that easily fooled.

'Natasha?' I heard Dad say. 'Did you hear me?'

'Sorry. Miles away.'

Dad smiled. 'It's been a big day, a long journey, lots to catch up on. Perhaps we should call it a night.'

Perhaps, I thought. But I knew why I wasn't listening.

'Dad,' I said, 'I heard you on the phone earlier. Who's Clarisse?'

Dad's face fell. 'What were you doing listening?'

I frowned. 'You were only in the next room, Dad. You were hardly quiet.'

'But I was speaking French.'

'Newsflash, Dad, I can speak some French too. And that's only some of the stuff I've learned in the last few years.' I couldn't have been more pointed if I'd said, 'You left, and I'm not the same as I was when I was ten.'

Despite himself, Dad was impressed. He chuckled, then remembered what I'd overheard.

'Look, *ma belle*, this isn't how I wanted to tell you.'

'Tell me what?'

'Clarisse is my girlfriend. We live together in Marseille. She wants to come out to Geneva. She's dying to meet you.'

CHAPTER 4
NELL

I didn't mean to be selfish but Hetal being away for the summer was a royal pain in my ass. Not so much Sasha. I mean, I'd miss them both equally, but Hetal was on my mum's list of approved friends and Sasha wasn't. Neither was Cam.

So now my main focus for the summer was how to get out of the house, preferably while keeping Mum happy. But also, what was I going to do with my time? Hetal's away, Sasha's away and Cam was (unhappily) stuck in a hardware store during normal opening hours. Did I rely too much on my friends for my life? So what? Lots of other people do and that's not unhealthy right? But I needed to think up something. Anything.

My mind often races from the moment I wake

up. Sometimes I feel like it's been galloping along while I've been asleep as well, so I wake up feeling tired and go to sleep feeling tired and can never seem to quite escape the thinking. Always thinking. Always worrying. Mum's got that saying, you know the one: worry is like a rocking chair, it never gets you anywhere but it gives you something to do. It's on a sign above the hob in the kitchen. I'm not sure I really get it. I mean, it's not like I need something to do. It feels more like I'm strapped into the rocking chair and someone is pushing away on the curved foot, forcing my mind to fly along at a hundred miles an hour. I feel like screaming, 'Stop the chair, I want to get off!'

I opened my eyes and looked round my room. It was five thirty and the sun was already streaming in through the gap in my curtains. I couldn't get up. It would disturb Mum, then she'd know I was awake early, then she'd get worried, then she'd be On My Case even more. If that were possible. No, I must carry on being a Perfectly Normal and Average Teenager. Hetal tells me that the average time a teenager wakes up is 9.47 a.m. I turned over and tried to get back to sleep.

I wondered how Sasha was getting on. She flew out and, despite a quick message saying she'd got there OK, I'd heard nothing. I wondered if Cam had heard more. She might have done. They are closer friends, those two. Perhaps they all have a three-way message going on. Without me. Oh, I annoy myself sometimes. Of course they don't. And even if they did, it wouldn't mean anything, would it? I mean, I've got one with Hetal, but that doesn't mean I like her better than the rest, it just means we have different sorts of conversations. Oh crap. I'm never going to get to sleep now. And I need a wee.

I crept out of bed, out of my room and along the corridor. Mum shot out of her room, hair a mess and looking startled.

'Are you OK? Everything alright?' she gabbled.

'I'm fine,' I replied. 'Needed the loo, that's all.'

She visibly relaxed. 'Righto, great.' And disappeared back to bed.

Man, my mum's a stress-head.

By nine o'clock I was ready to scream. What was I going to do with my day?

'I bumped into Hetal's grandmother yesterday,' said Mum.

'Right.' I felt a flush creep up my neck. I hope she didn't give me away. I'm not sure what about, it's just I've dodged about quite a bit, and I can't quite remember where I've said I've been, and where I've actually been. If you see what I mean.

'She said that Hetal's been invited to a very prestigious science camp for the summer.'

I nodded.

'She was clearly very proud of her. That's quite something, isn't it?'

I nodded again.

'I also went up to the hardware store to get some soft closers for the doors. And I saw that Cam in there. You know, Jackie and John's foster-child. She looks like a real wild one, that one. Bright pink hair *and* a nose ring. Can you believe it? And on the till as well.'

I wished she'd stop talking about Cam. I wished I could tell her the truth. That Cam was my friend and that Mum was wrong, wrong, wrong about her. That you can't judge a person by their situation or the colour of their hair.

But I didn't. I just sat quietly, picking away at the edges of my croissant. There was no point. Once Mum made her mind up about someone, there was no changing it.

'So, what are you going to do today?' said Mum. 'It's a shame Hetal's leaving this morning.'

You're telling me.

'I thought I'd walk into town,' I said.

'What? On your own? I'm not sure I like the idea.'

'I'll be OK. I need a few bits anyway.'

'Well,' Mum offered, 'perhaps I'll come in with you. Give you some company.'

I could barely think because of the screaming in my head. I needed some space, I needed some time to myself.

'You're OK, Mum,' I said as evenly as I could. Please, would she drop it. Please.

She looked at me hard for a second. I remembered the article I'd read about how to appear truthful. Look them straight in the eye and whatever you do, don't guilty-grin.

It must have worked cos Mum said, 'Oh alright then, but don't be too long.'

I'd left the house within the minute, before Mum had time to change her mind. I walked into town, wondering where I was going to go and what I was going to do. The library wasn't open, so I couldn't hang out there and I was totally flat broke, so I couldn't even treat myself to a lippy or a milkshake. As I walked up the street, looking in all the shop windows, full of seaside-y kitchenware and Devon fudge for the tourists, I came to the deli. I love the smell of that place. The window was full of pastries and cooked meats, pies and pots of olives. A notice was stuck on the window:

Job vacancy for serving staff, part-time, some weekends, excellent rate of pay. Apply within.

What a great job for someone that would be, I thought. I was about to move on when I stopped. What about for me? I needed something to do over the summer, something that got me out of the house, something that would give me money. Why did I always assume that things weren't for me? Why couldn't I do that job? I thought of Hetal's nani and remembered what we'd promised. No regrets. There was no harm in asking about it, was there?

I pushed open the door, the bell jangling over my head. The shop was warm and packed with shoppers. I queued up behind them, my hand clammy and my mouth dry. I was going to have to ask about the job in front of a shop full of people. I looked to see who was behind the counter. A middle-aged woman was laughing with a customer while counting slices of ham into a paper bag. She didn't look too scary.

The queue in front of me cleared and I found myself standing at the counter. Where was the friendly-looking lady who'd been serving?

'Can I help you?' said a boy. He was a touch taller than me. His eyes seemed to be laughing.

'Um,' I said. I couldn't ask him about the job. I'd die of embarrassment.

'Just some bread please?' I managed.

'Which sort?' he asked, waving his hand towards an overwhelmingly huge number of different breads. I mean, come on, who needs that many varieties?

'That one,' I said, pointing. I didn't care. I just needed to leave with my dignity intact.

He reached down a loaf, wrapped it in paper and said, 'That's £2.90.'

It was then I remembered. I hadn't any money. My face burned.

'I'm sorry,' I said. 'I've forgotten my purse.'

I turned and pushed my way through the sea of women, wrenched open the door and fled down the street. So much for my sodding dignity.

It took a cup of strong coffee with sugar before I felt better. Cam sorted me out, pulling out a box I could sit on behind the counter while she worked the till.

'Thanks,' she said to a customer. 'See you again.'

She turned to me. The hardware shop was poorly lit and packed to the ceiling with every screw, nut, bolt and tool there was. 'Where's the bread then?'

'I didn't have any money so I legged it.'

Cam threw back her pink head and roared with laughter.

'So pleased I can brighten your day,' I said. The caffeine and sugar rush had stopped the shaking and I was starting to (maybe) see the funny side.

'So, are you going back?'

'You're kidding. I'm never going back down that street, let alone back in the shop to ask for a job.'

'What? But you've got to,' said Cam. 'Remember the rule – no regrets.'

'Well, I'm full of regret,' I retorted. 'I regret going in there, regret not asking about the job and regret not having any money.'

Cam chuckled. 'You gotta turn it around. Otherwise, those regrets are what you're left with.'

The shop door dinged and I looked over at the customer coming in. It was my mum. And I was here, with Cam. I ducked down under the counter, right by Cam's feet. She frowned at me, but looked back up over the counter and said nothing. I could hear my mum asking about non-slip mats to go under rugs. It must be for the rug in the hall, it was always moving when we walked on it. Cam took

39

her to where they were in the shop and then came back to the counter.

'What do you think you're doing?' she hissed down at me. But Mum was back, clutching her new mat.

'How much is this one?' I heard her ask. She's got a funny voice she puts on in shops. I pulled back further under the counter.

Cam told her, took her money and tied up the mat with some string so it would be easier to carry. The shop bell dinged again as she left.

'She's gone,' said Cam. 'You can come out.'

I crawled out, dusting myself down. Cam just stood there, a funny look on her face.

'So? Want to tell me what that was all about?'

If I'm honest, I really didn't.

CHAPTER 5
HETAL

I waved as Mum and Dad drove away down the long track. Part of me wanted to run after them and beg them to take me home. They were going slowly enough for me to catch them if I ran fast. I estimated what speed they were travelling at, and how fast I'd have to accelerate and to what constant speed in order to catch up with them. By which time, of course, they'd disappeared round the bend.

I let my hand drop to my side. No point in waving any more. I'd just look stupid. Glancing around, I checked no one was watching. There were a few others about, saying goodbye to parents, checking maps and comparing schedules, but no one was paying any attention to me. The main reception was in an oversized cabin, set in a clearing

41

among tall trees. Every now and again, a fir cone fell and clonked off the roof. I calculated the odds of being hit on the head by a falling pine cone (pretty low) and the chance of being concussed by it (pretty high, as they sounded solid).

Picking up my rucksack, I went inside to check in. Twenty minutes later I'd been allocated to the Ada Lovelace cabin, to Team Cobalt, and had every second of the next couple of weeks accounted for in a rather impressive timetable. I was itching to colour-code it.

Searching through the pile of papers I'd been given, I found the map, checked where my cabin was and set off down a track through the trees. The sun was shining, the ground dappled by the shade from the leaves and the track was dry and springy underfoot. There were half a dozen cabins and Ada Lovelace was one of the ones furthest from the centre of camp. Each cabin had its own path peeling off from the main track. My cabin looked like the others, wood with an overhanging roof with a shallow pitch. Inside there was an entrance where boots and coats could be stored. Through the door was a large dormitory, with bathrooms at the far end. A huddle of girls was gathered at one side, all watching something on a phone. My heart gave a leap. Maybe there would be wifi.

Six beds each side, so twelve girls were going to be sleeping in here. I glanced down the rows. There was only one bed that hadn't been claimed yet. I hitched my backpack further up onto my shoulder and walked over to it, lowering my bag carefully down. The springs squeaked in complaint at the weight. Perhaps I hadn't needed to bring all my textbooks.

'Hi there,' said one of the girls in the huddle. 'You must be the twelfth – I'm Maddy.'

'Hi, I'm Hetal.'

Maddy quickly introduced everyone else, but I couldn't take in all their names. I smiled at them all, before they turned back to crowd round the screen. Feeling awkward, I decided to unpack my stuff. Each bed had its own bedside table and small wardrobe. With that done, I spent a bit of time studying the timetable, but truth was, I wasn't sure what I should do. For something that was supposed to be #NoRegrets, I felt like I had more regrets being here than I did at home. Things I'd rather be doing right now:

- Having a lie-in at home
- Chatting to Nani
- Homework

Perhaps I needed to be more positive. Things that I'd not prefer to be doing:

- Any kind of dental work
- Most of the challenges on that celebrity TV show
- Fighting a bear

Crap, I was missing home. I pulled out my phone.

Me: *Hey, at camp. Nice place but I miss you guys.*
Cam: *Of course you do – you're only human! x*
Nell: *I'm missing you too. Come home and we'll hang out x*
Sasha: *Don't you dare go home. Get off your phone and go make some geeky friends x*

I grinned. Sasha was right. It was the newness that felt weird. I had to give this a proper shot or, despite taking the plunge and coming to science camp, I'd still be left with regrets. Which would be ironic.

The timetable said there was an optional session before tea, so I grabbed my jumper and headed back towards the door.

'You going to the biochemistry lecture?' called Maddy.

'Yes, thought it sounded interesting,' I said.

'Great.' Maddy jumped up. 'I'll come too.'

Maddy was short with frizzy hair and the most enormous glasses I think I've ever seen. They made her look like an owl. Sort of.

'I've been totally freaking out since I got here,' she said. 'What if I don't know enough, or know the wrong stuff, or it's been a big mistake and I shouldn't even be here? I mean, if it had been sports camp, I'd known for certain they'd got it wrong. Do these legs look athletic to you?' She stuck out a leg in front of her. It might not have been the longest leg in the world statistically speaking but it looked fine to me. Thankfully, she carried on without waiting for a reply. Or drawing breath. 'But science. I love it. Total dream come true. And now I'm here, I'm freaking out. Brains, huh? Can't live with them, can't live without them.'

She was talking at a million miles an hour. Not that miles per hour is the correct unit of measurement for speaking. Perhaps it should be words per minute, or syllables per second. Anyway, she was fast and I was only catching one word in three unless I really concentrated.

'So, biochemistry...' I said.

'Yeah, love biochemistry. Feels like knowing all those facts about chemicals and reactions is really useful because it's applied to real stuff – like actual people and illnesses and micro-organisms. Reckon there's some interesting developments to come still in that field. I read in the *New Scientist* the other week that there's loads of small research labs, all on the brink of going to clinical trials for a whole load of different therapies. Wouldn't it be totally awesome to be the one who came up with a cure for cancer or MS or something?'

She didn't wait for an answer.

'Anyway, my mum says I always talk too much. But I haven't, have I? I mean, we're having a conversation, right? About biochemistry. So, what do you think?'

I was about to reply, when she pointed. 'Look, I think this is it. We're here.'

The Woodland Theatre was a circular clearing in the trees, with a ring of rough wooden benches around a campfire, which wasn't lit. A few other people were already there, sat in groups of two or three. A woman was standing in the middle, dressed in jeans and a checked shirt.

'Come on in, grab a seat. We'll get started in a minute.'

Maddy and I walked round to the far side and sat equidistant between two groups. We couldn't have been further from other people if we'd tried.

'That's Dr Angela Hoffman,' whispered Maddy, her face flushed. 'She's got two PhDs and has been recognised by the UN for the humanitarian applications of her research. Isn't she just wonderful?'

I looked at Dr Angela Hoffman and wondered what on earth she was doing leading an optional session at a camp for teenagers.

'OK,' said Dr Angela. 'I think that's probably everyone. We'll make a start then. Welcome to the first in the series of talks on biochemistry. We'll be looking at some theory, some case studies and finishing up with a look at career paths, should any of you be interested.'

I was hooked from the moment she opened her mouth. The hour passed like it was on fast forward.

'Thank you all for coming, and I'll see you here tomorrow, same time, same place. If I haven't scared you off.'

The only way I knew for certain that an hour had passed was that I had a numb bum and the sun had dipped slightly in the sky.

Dr Angela was chatting to a group as Maddy and I left the clearing.

'She was just amazing!' I said. 'The way she made the connection between theory and how to apply it, well, it was mind-blowing. I can't wait for her next session. Looks like it's every day, just before the evening meal. I'm not missing any of them. I mean. Just wow.'

'Alright, alright, let a girl get a word in edgeways,' said Maddy.

I looked at her incredulously. Talk about the pot calling the kettle black. But she was grinning.

'Got you,' she said, nudging me. I grinned back.

'Come on,' I said. 'Let's go and find the canteen. I'm starving.'

We walked together along the springy, bark-chip path towards the smell of garlic bread and baked lasagne, when I realised it had been ninety minutes since I'd last thought about home.

'You know,' said Maddy, 'every year, the science camp awards prizes to the people they think are the top students here.'

'How do you know?' I asked. I'd done a pretty thorough job of reading all the literature, on-line and physical, and nothing had been said about awards.

'My older sister came a few years back,' said Maddy.

'How do they decide? Are there exams?' As much as I loved an exam, I felt that I'd done my fair share this year and wasn't in a massive rush to sit any more just yet.

'No, no exams. Just based on general aptitude and likeliness to go far.'

It sounded like the most unscientific way imaginable which felt kind of paradoxical. I'd have to add it into my list of favourite paradoxes:

1. This statement is false.
2. No one likes the popular kids.
3. The classic: you need experience for a job but need a job to get experience.

'There's a big ceremony on the last night and everything,' Maddy was saying.

I stopped thinking about paradoxes with a jolt as a shiver of excitement zipped up and down my spine. Talking about prizes and ceremonies and winning brought out the competitive side of my nature. I wanted to win an award, no matter what.

CHAPTER 6
CAM

The hardware shop was dark, even on the sunniest of days. Natural light tried to get in through a roof light in the ceiling at the back of the shop, but that was so fuzzed up with spiders' webs that it didn't have much success. The walls were lined from floor to ceiling with racking, all stacked with tiny boxes of screws and packets of vacuum-cleaner bags, Kilner jars for home preserving and rubber washers for leaky taps. If I was the sensitive type, I'd have said the shop was claustrophobic. The passageways between the columns of stock were narrow and a tall stepladder was needed to reach the stuff at the top.

After a week, I was getting into the swing of life working full time in the shop. I'd arrive with Papa John to open up and sort through the post, usually an assortment of bills and brochures, then onto the first brew of the day. Papa John wasn't one to forget his northern roots. Part of his identity was drinking tea that looked more like the creosote we sold for preserving fences. Then he'd disappear into the back to do accounts or to ring suppliers or check on stock, and I'd be left to amuse myself behind the till. I'd started out by sorting the counter into some sort of order, then progressed to the higgledy-piggledy display of bargain trade-paint. Earlier in the week, I'd added my own touch to the marketing campaign with a slogan that read 'Who said you can't whitewash it?' handprinted on a piece of cardboard I'd found out back which I propped up next to the pots of lime paint.

Papa John had given me free rein, which was odd – I wouldn't have trusted me with his business. At lunchtime, I had half an hour off and I'd bolt for the door, like a bird from a cage, and head down to the bench on the quay, eating my sandwiches there and staying until the very last second before legging it back up the hill to the shop.

It wasn't that I hated it. It was just I could think of better things to be doing. I would have been lonely if it hadn't been for Nell, who kept popping in and sitting on the box behind the counter. I kept pushing her to go back to the deli and see about that job. But she wouldn't. And she wouldn't tell me why she'd hidden when her mum came into the shop either. That was proper weird. I didn't push her. She'd looked terrified. I'm guessing she wasn't supposed to be out, or was supposed to be somewhere else. Her mum's uber-protective, and has gone into hyper-drive since Nell's accident.

In between customers, once I'd tidied up, there wasn't a whole lot to do, which left me with a lot of thinking time. I tried to find things to do – even brought in a crossword book to take away some of the mind-numb – but it was no good. I kept thinking about what would happen after I left Papa John and Jackie. I've been with them for three years, which is the longest I've been with any foster-family by *miles*. My mum died when I was eight and I lived with my gran for a bit until she got too sick to have me. Funny thing is I never usually worry about not having any 'proper' family. Perhaps what set me off was that I'd just done my GCSEs, and was thinking about what I'd do next. Whatever it was, I couldn't get the question out of my head: who is my real dad? And by real, I mean birth father. Papa John was only going to be there for as long as he was paid to be. And when I got to eighteen, I could choose to stay or move on. But what if they wanted me to move on before then? Even if I stayed till I was twenty-one, in five years' time, I'd still be on my own.

Since finishing my exams everything felt different. My future was approaching fast and I couldn't see what it was going to look like.

But I had a birth father. That was blood. There was no end to that. Where was he? Who was he? Was he still alive, or had he gone the same way as my mum, so broken by drugs that his body had given up on him?

I tried to stop thinking about him and for a few days I managed it. I spring-cleaned the shop, washing the windows and hooking down the cobwebs that hung between the shelving units.

I had managed three whole days without thinking about my real father when Jackie gave me a form to fill in from the doctors.

'Now you're sixteen, it's probably time you started filling forms in for yourself,' she said.

She's getting me ready to leave, I thought. Perhaps this is a hint, perhaps they're going to break it gently to me over the summer. Still time to settle into a new foster home before college – ideal time, really, if you think about it.

The form was fine at first, just name and address, easy stuff, but it asked about diseases in your family. I guessed that my foster-family's medical history wasn't what the doctor was after.

'Jackie? What should I put?' I asked. I didn't know what diseases, if any, my blood family had.

'Just tick "don't know",' said Jackie, as she carried on folding the washing.

I ticked 'don't know' and handed it into the doctors on my way to work the next day, but I couldn't stop thinking about it. I didn't know. I didn't know if my father had a condition that was hereditary. Didn't know if something inside me was a ticking time bomb. What if I had something that was easy to fix, if only I knew about it? Don't be ridiculous, I told myself. I'm perfectly healthy. There's nothing wrong with me. But the hours in the shop gave me mulling time and I couldn't escape the what ifs.

So, one day, when the shop was quiet, I logged on to the internet using the main computer on the counter which we usually used to find out how long replacement stock would take, or how much our competitors were selling stuff for.

I knew two things about my father. His name and where he'd met my mum. My mum hadn't put him on my birth certificate and the social workers never knew who he was. My mum had been so against 'the social' that she hadn't told them a thing. But she'd told me his name. And once, when she was sober, she told me all about the summer they'd spent together. I typed in his name: Phil Mirren. A list of links appeared: Twitter, Linkedin and Facebook.

How would I know which was him? I scrolled and clicked and searched. There were some which I could ignore immediately, either too young or too old. After an hour, I'd looked through all the social-media ones – there was only a website left. I clicked on a link to a Phil Mirren business page. On the page were tiny photos of the people running the company. I scanned down, looking for Phil Mirren's name. But it wasn't the name that stopped me. It was the photo. It was of a middle-aged, slightly balding man in a suit with a solemn face, as in all business photos. But he had my nose. And chin. Or rather I had his.

Could that be him? It had to be.

My mouth was dry, my fingers trembling, as I tried to find out more about him. Now I knew where he worked, I'd be able to figure out roughly where in the country he lived. Not that I was going to do anything about it. Of course I wasn't. I was just curious. There was no harm in looking. Researching a bit.

The business was based in Plymouth. That was only just over an hour away on the bus. Not far. Which made it feel a bit more real. A bit more possible.

'How's it going?' said Papa John as he came into the shop from the back office.

I jumped. I'd forgotten I was supposed to be working. I minimised the screen and started looking at washers.

'Great,' I said brightly. 'No problems.'

'It's a bit quiet this afternoon.' He looked around the shop. No one had been in for half an hour.

'It'll pick up,' I said. I clicked through from the supplier's website to another one. I just needed to look busy, that's all.

'Well, I'll be out back if you need me.'

'OK.'

He disappeared through the office door. When he'd gone I pulled up the details about Phil Mirren again.

What should I do? Nothing of course. The guidelines are very clear when it comes to contact.

Only through official channels, and only if both parties agree to it.

I texted Nell. *Hey, think I've found my real father online. Should I contact him?*

Nell: *What? Don't do anything. I'll be right there.*

I stared at the man who looked like an older, maler version of me. It was weird. So weird. Within five minutes, Nell had burst through the shop door, the bell jangling loudly.

'I came as fast as I could.'

'Honestly, you shouldn't have rushed. It's not like someone's died,' I said. But I was glad she was there. Nell's super-cautious. She would be just the right person to stop me doing anything stupid.

'So?' said Nell. 'How do you know it's him?'

I pointed to the picture on the screen. She looked at it closely.

'He's the spit of you,' she said finally. I knew this. I had eyes. His eyes actually.

'I feel like I want to know more about him,' I said. And I did. I could feel my inner stalker dusting herself off. Come on, Nell. Here's your chance to talk some sense into me. Save me from myself.

'What do you want to know?'

'All sorts. The big stuff, the small stuff. Everything. I was only looking cos I was curious. But now I've seen him…' I paused to work out what I actually did feel. 'He seems real. Like there's a connection. Does that sound crazy?'

Nell shook her head. 'Not crazy at all.'

'What do I do?'

Nell looked at me closely. 'I guess the question you have to answer is: which would you regret the most – finding out something you didn't like about him, or never knowing him and missing out on the possibility of him being a good thing?'

Great. So much for Nell being a restraining influence.

CHAPTER 7
SASHA

We went to pick Clarisse up from the airport. It was blistering. It seems that Geneva in August has two weather variations: hot and hotter. And this was hotter. I was constantly on the lookout for the next air-conditioned room, or car, or shop. How people could function wearing the clothes they wore, I had no idea. As we waited in the arrivals lounge, I tried to imagine what Clarisse would look like. Probably a French, chic version of my mum. Perhaps a bit older, as my mum's a few years younger than my dad. Dad said she worked in sales, that she'd lived in Marseille all her life, and that they'd been together for nearly a year. And he hadn't thought to mention this sooner?

'Clarisse! *Par ici*! Over here!' Dad called. I

looked to where he was waving. A trickle of people was coming through the double doors. There was a couple with a baby, an elderly gentleman and a young woman with enormous heels and massive sunglasses. Clarisse couldn't be any of those.

Dad pushed his way past people waiting, went up to the young woman and kissed her. As in really kissed. As in, get a room kissed. So, two things. One: that must be Clarisse. And two: gross. Not her exactly. Them. Together. Just no.

I waited a bit. They clearly didn't need me bounding up and wrecking what looked like a fairly passionate reunion. (Did I mention the gross thing?)

I decided that I'd wait it out further away, so I walked back through the lounge, picked a chair right under the air-conditioning outlet and got out my phone.

Me: *Guys, you'll never guess what, my dad's gf is really young. As in Really Young.*

I waited for their replies, scrolling through photos while I did so. They all must be busy. Cam usually replied quickly cos she was bored in the shop, but I guessed Hetal was arm-deep in chemicals or Bunsen burners or something. I wondered what Nell was up to. It felt weird not to know. I didn't like it. A massive wave of homesickness engulfed me. I was sat in some swelteringly hot airport missing being with my friends because I'd decided to spend time with my dad, who was currently kissing the face off a girl who looked literally half his age. My dad may be having the summer of his life but I sure as hell wasn't.

Dad and Clarisse walked up. Dad was holding her hand, which was weird cos they looked like they could be father and daughter. Like she was my older sister. New waves of gross hit me.

'I'll be in the car,' I said and walked off towards the door. Dad did a low-level protest call after me, but it's not his thing to make a public scene. Wouldn't sit well with the ultra-cool thing he's got going on.

'She'll come round,' I thought he said in French. Come round, my arse. Didn't matter which way you dressed it up, the age gap was just freaky. And I wasn't going to change my mind.

I stood by the car, melting, and wishing I'd gone somewhere air-conditioned to make my point, when Dad and Clarisse walked up. Dad unlocked the car. I got in the passenger seat. Dad gave me the evils. I gave them right back with an added twist of 'What are you going to do about it?' He apologised to Clarisse, who elegantly tucked herself into the seat behind Dad. He gently shut the door for her and got into the driver's seat, still frowning my way.

I turned my head and looked out of the window. None of this was my fault. He could have said before I decided to come to Geneva. It would have been easy: 'Say, want to know something? I've got a girlfriend and she's like half my age. You cool with this?'

And I would have said, 'Hell no, you complete weirdo,' and I would have stayed at home. With my mum. Who is the right age. And my friends, who were cool with me leaving them for the summer, despite us having made a ton of plans.

I watched as the tall city buildings turned to smaller suburban ones, until finally buildings were less frequent than fields. Dad had put the radio on to cover the awkward silence, which totally didn't work. Out of the corner of my eye, I had a look at Clarisse. She still had her sunglasses on and she was typing quickly on her phone, her long nails tapping on the screen. She wore cream linen trousers which were annoyingly crease-free. She'd just been on a flight? Where was the justice in the world? Why hadn't she arrived looking like me? Hot, sticky and wearing her holiday clothes. She looked up and caught me watching her.

Now call me overly-sensitive, but if you were meeting your boyfriend's teenage daughter for the first time, you might try cracking a smile, or saying hi, or asking about school, or anything really. But no. Clarisse didn't smile. She lifted her head, looked around, then back to her phone. Not a flicker of a smile. Not a flicker of anything. She didn't even *see* me. Complete disinterest. Stunning.

Well, two can play at that game. I pulled out my phone. Nell had replied.

Nell: *How young? Surely she can't be that young.*
Me: *Like she could be my older sister.*
Nell: *Nooooo! Is she nice?*

I thought about it for a minute. What she was like didn't come into it. She was too young. End of.

Me: *No. She isn't.*
Nell: *Ouch. That's going to be one long summer.*
Me: *Yeah, cheers for that!*

Dad pulled into the apartment car park.

'I've got to pop to the office. I won't be too long. You've got a key to get in, haven't you, Sasha?'

I looked at Dad. He was abandoning me with

her? I glanced back at Clarisse. I couldn't read her expression behind her enormous sunglasses. Can't imagine she'd be that impressed being left with me either.

'Yeah, sure, Dad,' I said, digging it out of my pocket. He was doing what he did best. When the going got tough, he left. Classic Dad.

We stood and watched as he pulled out of the car park and away down the road.

'Come on,' I said to Clarisse, before walking towards the entrance, leaving her to haul her own bag. I could let her in, show her the place, but there was no way I was going to make her feel welcome.

I walked up the stairs, listening to her bumping her bag up the steps and cursing quietly in French. This would crease up those linen trousers a bit.

I held the door open nearly long enough for her and went in to make myself a cold drink, before sitting down on the sofa in the breeze of the air-conditioning unit.

Clarisse kicked open the door and I felt a twinge of envy. How was she staying upright, kicking a door and standing on one foot in those heels and *still* looking amazing? She dragged her bags in and dropped them in the hallway, letting the door slam shut behind her. She pushed her sunglasses on top of her head, her eyes looking around the apartment, taking in the doors to the balcony, the small kitchen and me on the sofa.

She walked over to my bedroom door and looked in.

'That room's mine,' I said.

She didn't flinch, but walked on to the next door and went inside. I sat on the sofa, too mad to drink my drink, too mad to read my book. I was stuck here, babysitting Dad's girlfriend. I could be out somewhere now, doing something, but instead I was stuck here with her.

A few minutes later she came back out again for her bags.

'My dad didn't say you were young,' I said before I could help myself. 'How old are you exactly?'

Clarisse looked at me, her dark eyes glittering, her red lips pursed. 'Well,' she said in a thick French accent, 'your dad didn't tell me he had such a spoilt brat as a daughter.' She pulled her bag across the sitting area and into Dad's room.

Nell was right. This was going to be one hell of a long summer.

I downed my drink, picked up my phone and sunglasses and walked out of the apartment. How dare she talk to me like that? The rage bubbled under my skin as I walked down the hill to the restaurant by the lake. It was nearly empty, the sun was overhead and all sensible people were indoors.

I found a shady corner right next to the lake edge. I looked over the low wall into the water below. It was crystal clear and there were large fish swimming in and out of the weeds.

'Hello again,' said a voice. It was the Greek god of a boy.

'Hi.' It must have been the adrenaline flooding my blood after the spoilt-brat comment, but I felt invincible. I turned up the wattage on my smile.

'What can I get you?'

'What do you recommend?' I was flirting, but it felt fun. This was my holiday after all. 'I'm after a long, cold drink.' I said the words slow.

'I have just the thing.' He walked away to the bar. I picked up some breadcrumbs off the table and dropped them into the water, watching the big, gulpy mouths of the fish as they surfaced and sucked them down.

'Try this.' He presented a tall glass to me with a flourish. If the waiter in Alley Cats back home had done that we'd have laughed ourselves sick, but here? Here it was fine. More than fine.

'What is it?' It was deep purple and had a straw sticking out of it.

'Try it. If you do not like it, it is on the house.'

I sucked on the straw. It was gorgeous. 'Mm, delicious!'

'You are more than welcome,' he said, before disappearing off into the kitchen.

The drink really was wonderful. It had a hint of fizz and the colour must have come from something grapey but, as for exactly what was in it, I didn't know and didn't care. I sat and sipped, my head feeling lighter. By the end of the drink, I still didn't feel like going back to face Clarisse, so I ordered another and sat drinking and watching the sun dipping in the sky.

'Is your friend not with you today?' asked the waiter, as he laid the table next to me, ready for the evening.

'What? You mean my dad?' I laughed. 'No, he's at work today.'

'Well, I had guessed, but didn't want to presume. You aren't from round here, are you?'

And there was me thinking my French was impeccable. I grinned. 'No, is it that obvious?'

He shrugged. 'A lucky guess, that is all. Have you walked along the lakeside yet?'

When I shook my head, he gasped in faux-shock, making me laugh again.

'A travesty. You must see it. It is gorgeous. *Peut-être*, on my next day off, you would allow me to show you our fabulous lake?'

My stomach flipped. This was more than just waiter/customer banter now, right?

'My name's Pierre, by the way.'

'Sasha.'

'*Enchanté*, Sasha.'

I paused for a moment, before saying, 'OK, sure.' Why not? He might be a couple of years older than me, but that was nothing compared to Dad and Clarisse. 'I'd like that.'

CHAPTER 8
NELL

It had taken me two days to build up the courage to walk past the deli again. And another two days after that in order to stop in front of the window. The advert was still there. I was desperate for the job but also wished the advert would disappear so that I didn't have to try. In total, I walked past the deli twelve times and stopped twice. The food in the window looked fabulous. The pork pies and pasties, which must have been made in store, always got me right in the nostrils.

I bet if I went in now, he wouldn't even remember me. Bet I was just one in a blur of customers. Bet I was over-thinking it, that there wasn't really anything to be embarrassed about, that if only I could open the door, walk in and say, 'I've come about the job,' all my worries would evaporate. I put my hand out to push the door open, but changed my mind at the last moment and walked away down the street. Stupid. Stupid. Why couldn't I do this? It seemed every time I tried, my mind rebelled, or was it my body? I was going to have a life crammed with regrets at this rate, never mind a summer. I'd already crashed and burned. Still here to cringe another day. I was going to do it. I was going to do it right now.

I made an old lady jump as I spun round and marched back up the hill. I was going to do this. And it wouldn't matter if I didn't get the job. At least I would have tried. It would be one less regret in my sea of regrets.

I pushed the door hard, the bell jangling. It was mid-afternoon, the early morning and lunchtime rushes were over and the shop was empty, apart from the woman I'd seen last time, who was busy wiping down the metal surfaces. There was loud music playing. She didn't look up. She seemed to be dancing and … singing?

'Hi,' I said loudly. We were the only two people in the shop. It wouldn't get much better than this. It was now or never.

'Oh, sorry love, didn't hear you come in,' she

said, turning the music down. 'But you can't listen to Aretha quietly, can you?'

I must have looked confused.

'Aretha Franklin? Greatest singer of all time?' She looked at me expectantly. 'Never mind. What can I get you?'

'I've come about the job?' I said. 'The one in the window.'

The woman beamed and wiped her hands on the cloth. 'Great! So, tell me a bit about yourself.'

It was like I'd been plunged into a vat of dry ice. If I'd been tapped with a hammer I'd have shattered.

The woman smiled at me encouragingly.

'Um,' I said. I wouldn't employ me. A kid who forgets how to speak. Making informal chit-chat with the customers is a vital part of the job. Come on, you idiot. Just say something. Anything.

'How about start with your name?' said the woman.

'Sorry. Yes. Of course. My name. It's Nell. Nell Cooper.'

You could have wrung me out I was sweating so badly.

'Hi, Nell,' said the woman. 'I'm Wendy. If you don't mind me asking, how old are you?'

71

'Sixteen.'

'And why do you want to work in my little deli?'

'Well. Um.' Why did I want to work here? I wanted to get out of the house, get some money and this was the first job I'd seen. I wasn't too sure that was what Wendy wanted to hear.

'Your deli always smells fantastic,' I said. What? I want to work here because it *smells* nice? Dig a hole and bury me now.

I was totally expecting her to say thanks but no thanks, or I'll keep you in mind, or something else that basically meant get out of my shop, you deluded individual.

'OK. The hours are quite flexible. There will always be someone else working with you and you get to take home any food that's left over at the end of the day.'

Eh, what?

'Have you got any questions?'

Yes. About a billion.

'Are you offering me the job?'

'Yes.'

'Cool.'

There was silence for a moment.

'Thanks,' I said finally. 'When do I start?'

'How about tomorrow? You need to be here for

seven. We bake a lot of our own bread and pasties, and there's quite a rush of people collecting lunchtime sandwiches on their way to work, so it's an early start. But you should be all done by two.'

'Great. I'll see you tomorrow then?'

'Tomorrow.'

I pulled open the shop door and stepped outside, the air cool on my face. I felt like I was floating. I'd done it. I'd been in and asked and I'd got the job. For a split second I had a feeling of pure joy. A grin spread across my face. I should have asked about pay, and what days I was going to work and what I was expected to do, and wear.

The joy was souring, like yellow paint with a blob of black dripped in. What was I going to wear? And what would Mum say? I'd got a job. I'd not even told her I was thinking about one. Surely she would be pleased? Most parents are pleased when their teenagers get jobs. But Mum wasn't most parents.

Over tea that night, I couldn't swallow my food properly. It kept getting stuck in my throat and I was having to sip water with every mouthful to get the stuff down.

Dad was busy talking about the price of fish.

Literally. He's a fish merchant, so that's pretty much all he talks about and all he smells of.

'I can't believe the price of fresh crab this last week,' he was saying. 'There must be a big posh do coming up in Salcombe because you can't get decent fresh crab for love nor money.'

Why anyone would offer love in exchange for fresh crab, or any crustacean for that matter, I had no idea. I kept shovelling my food. Mum watched what I ate closely. She'd heard that eating healthily can improve the outcome for amputees, but I suspected it didn't make much difference a year on. Still, like a lot of things, she couldn't let it go.

As a blob of chicken curry and rice scratched down my throat, I realised that this was my best chance to tell them about the job. Dad might be a helpful ally.

'I've got some good news.' I might as well give it my best shot. I smiled, stretching my face to try and look happy.

'Really?' said Dad.

'I've got a job.'

I kept smiling but inside I was screaming: brace, brace, brace.

'That's brilliant,' said Dad. 'Congratulations! I got a job when I was about your age and it was the best thing I could have done. Great fun and loads of experience.'

'But Ted,' said Mum, lowering her voice, as if there was something wrong with my hearing. 'Do you think it's a good idea for Nell? You know. Because of everything.'

'Yes, I do,' said Dad. 'I think it's great. So, Nell, what's the job?'

'It's serving at the deli in town. I start tomorrow.'

Mum was panicking but trying to hide it. Only she's crap at hiding it.

'The deli? What? With meat-cutting machines and raw meat and strangers coming into the shop all the time?'

'You mean customers, Mum?' I said.

'They're people you don't know, Nell, so strangers. They could follow you home after work. There's some really odd people around, you know.'

I rolled my eyes.

'And don't you look like that – you can't just go out and get a job without checking with us first. We have to know it's safe for you. The brain isn't mature till your early twenties. Who knows what sort of shop this is. Ted, back me up here.'

Dad looked trapped. Cornered, as ever, between us.

I pushed back my chair. 'It's alright. I don't need your permission, either of you. I was only telling you. I've got a job at the deli and I start work tomorrow. And there's nothing you can do or say that's going to change that.'

I turned and stomped out of the kitchen, slamming the door hard behind me, making all the pictures jiggle on the wall. Things were going to be awkward at home but I didn't care – I'd be out. At work.

CHAPTER 9
HETAL

On the second morning Team Cobalt were scheduled for a practical chemistry session. Fortunately, Maddy was on my team too, so we automatically became lab partners. We were testing the pH of a range of substances. As we racked up our test tubes and got out bottles of indicator solution and litmus paper, I made a list of the things we were testing. Some were going to be tricky because they were in solid form. Ideally, to test, the substance should be a liquid. I jotted down some ideas for how we could solve this.

Maddy and I worked hard, dissolving, testing and repeat-testing samples to check our accuracy. Most results were what we predicted, but one substance didn't behave in the way we expected. It didn't help that it was a blind test and neither me nor Maddy recognised the substance. We'd decided to dissolve it with water and test, but that gave different results from when we put indicator solution directly onto some of the substance in a test tube. We tested and retested. There was only one thing it could mean. It was reacting in some way to the water.

'Let's test it one last time before we let the session leader know,' I said. We worked at re-dissolving and testing again. As we waited for our results, the boy at the bench next to us got very excited.

'Hey, over here!' he called to the leader.

The man in the white lab coat at the front walked over to his bench.

'I reckon this one's different,' said the boy. 'I get different results if I dissolve it in water.'

The leader chuckled. 'Well done, Finn, good work. You've found my deliberate mistake. I was wondering who would spot it.'

We found it too, I wanted to say. *And we've triple-checked it.* But I didn't. I should have called out earlier. But it wasn't good science to guess before thoroughly testing. Maddy and I wrote up our results, ready to finish the experiment the following day.

That evening Josh, the camp leader, stood up

while we were finishing our meal. He tinged his glass for silence.

'I hope you've all had a good day today. And I hope those in the chemical testing session this morning have managed to get the smell of rotten eggs out of their hair.'

There was some laughing from a group on the far side of the dining area.

'So now you've all had a chance to settle in, we thought we'd start our daily awards, which all add towards the awards given at the end of camp, and are worthy of going on your CVs and being stuck to the fridge.'

More laughing. I didn't laugh, though. Awards aren't things to joke about.

'The daily award goes to someone who has done something outstanding that day, something that has impressed a member of the camp faculty.'

The room was silent. Which was hardly surprising. Science types like to know the criteria they are being tested on. It's like the reassurance of a tick-box list. But this seemed wishy-washy. How did you manage to do something 'outstanding'? Everyone here was the best in their geographical area. I'd done some investigating and I was the only person here from the whole of Devon.

'To kick things off, today's award, for spotting the anomaly in the pH testing, goes to Finn Gilbertson.'

I glanced over to Maddy. That was the guy who had tested once and called out on a hunch and got lucky. I watched as Finn left his friends and walked to the front while everyone applauded. I clapped. But only a bit. Perhaps at 30 per cent.

He was given a small star mounted on a tiny stand. Finn held it above his head in a fake celebration. My stomach churned. That should have been us. We'd found the same anomaly. It should have been me. And tomorrow it would be.

I stared hard at Finn as he walked past. He caught my eye and winked, before grinning and going back to his mates.

This game was on.

The next day, every session I was in, I shot my hand up. Question after question I got right. What's the chemical symbol for sodium carbonate? How do iron and sulphur react? What precautions should you take? I didn't get a single one wrong. It felt amazing.

At morning break, Maddy passed me a coffee.

'Here, drink this. Not that you need any

caffeine. You're totally acing it this morning. What's got into you?'

'Nothing.' I sipped the coffee. 'I just thought there wasn't any point in holding back, that's all.'

'You're after the award, aren't you?'

'What if I am?'

'Don't let that Finn get to you,' said Maddy. 'Just because he got the results ahead of us yesterday.'

But it was getting to me. Next session was the second half of our pH testing experiment. Maddy and I got out the equipment ready. I was itching to get started. I wanted to double-check our results, then write it up well before handing it in. The leader would see that we'd done the right thing. Surely then he'd acknowledge that by giving me the award?

That evening, after the biochemistry session, Maddy and I walked along to dinner. I could hardly eat a mouthful. What if I didn't get the award tonight? What if someone else had done something amazing in one of the other sessions? What if Finn won it again?

As Josh stood up, the room gradually quietened down. I could feel my pulse in my head.

'I hear from everyone that's it's been another excellent day today.'

He paused. 'Onto today's award. This award has been given to someone who has answered questions and put herself forward at every opportunity, really embracing taking part and impressing the leaders with her knowledge. Today's award goes to Hetal Badesha.'

I stood up as everyone applauded.

'Finn, could you come up and hand over the trophy to today's winner?'

I waited next to Josh as Finn weaved his way between tables, bringing the tiny award with him. It was mine for the next twenty-four hours.

Finn handed it over and I clutched it to my chest. 'Well done, Hetal, for putting your hand up and taking part.'

I glared at him. Josh had said 'impressing with her knowledge' but Finn had completely ignored *that* part. I'd watched fights at school and never understood why people end up punching each other. But, in that instant, I knew exactly how they felt. I wanted to use that trophy to inflict physical pain on that smarmy, know-it-all face of Finn Gilbertson.

CHAPTER 10
CAM

Nell had made me promise that I wouldn't rush into anything. She said it was like Pandora's box. Though I had no clue what that meant. It had been several days since I'd seen Phil Mirren's photo and I couldn't get his face out of my head. It had properly freaked me out when I'd dreamed about him, too. I couldn't be doing that all the time. I had to make a decision one way or the other. Perhaps a little message wouldn't hurt.

It was quiet late morning, as it usually was after the early morning rush of tradesmen getting their supplies for the day. Papa John had popped out to visit a supplier, so I had the place to myself. Or, more specifically, the computer to myself.

I clicked onto his business website and searched his name. Phil Mirren popped up. The company obviously had an open policy, as there were little contact buttons under each person's picture. At least the message would go straight to him. I clicked the 'contact me' button and a small inset screen came up, the cursor flashing. Some grey-out words read 'write your message here'.

My message. What would my message be?

Hi Dad, long time, never seen.

Perhaps not.

Hello Phil, I have some information about your daughter you might like to know.

Hm, sounds a bit too like a blackmail threat. I didn't want to come across as some kind of loser-freak.

In the end I wrote:

Hi, my name's Cam. You don't know me, but I'm your daughter. I'm 16. Would you like to meet up?

I read it through. Seemed OK. Friendly, but not too pushy. I'd given him some details, but not too many. And I'd left the ball in his court. If he said he didn't want to meet up, then that would be the end of it. And no regrets.

I pressed send. I wondered how long it would take for him to answer.

An error message pinged up. Message not delivered. I groaned. My nerves could not take this kind of crap.

I googled him again and searched for another way to contact him, but he was like a person from another century. I couldn't find a trace of him on any social-media site. The man must be a monk. Honestly, how did anyone survive like that?

I searched for the rest of the morning. When Papa John finally returned, I had exhausted every idea I had. I clicked the browser shut after deleting the history.

'Good morning, Papa John?' I asked. I nodded and smiled at the appropriate moments as he talked about new lines of screwdrivers and a deluxe range of power tools.

'I'm popping out for a sandwich. Do you want me to get you one?' I said when I'd had as much tool-chat as I could stomach.

'Yes, thanks, love.'

Walking down the street, the fresh air on my face and the sun warming my arms, life felt possible again. So what if I couldn't contact him via the internet? That was only one way to get in touch. Perhaps I needed to think differently. Think off-line, more real world. As I returned to the shop with two warm bacon butties in my hands, I knew what I had to do.

Papa John and I sat in the back office, mugs of

dark builder's tea and hot, drippy bacon rolls on the desk between us.

'Papa John?' I said, between mouthfuls. 'Could I have a day's holiday?'

His eyebrows shot up. Papa John may not be much of a talker, but what he doesn't say with words, he makes up for with his eyebrows. 'What for? Aren't you enjoying it?'

'I'm loving every second of it, obviously. It's every girl's dream to work in a hardware shop.'

Papa John snorted his tea.

'I mean,' I said, 'it's great. I could do with a day to go into Plymouth, that's all.'

He took a massive bite of his bacon roll and chewed. I waited patiently. You can't rush Papa John.

'OK. That's OK. How's Thursday?'

Thursday. Three days away. I'd have to wait three days.

'Sure,' I said. 'Thursday's great.'

That evening, I was sitting on our bench with Nell. It was weird being just the two of us. I was used to having the loudness of Sasha to bounce off and the well-researched insights from Hetal. I wondered if Nell was missing them too and was feeling a bit short-changed having to spend her summer with me.

'What are you planning to do on Thursday?' she asked.

I hadn't exactly figured out the details. Sometimes it played out in my head like a cheesy movie where I ran towards him and he hugged me and spun me round. I was annoyed that I even allowed that kind of cliché into my brain. But it was there – irritating the hell out of me with its persuasive rose-tintedness.

'I'm not sure,' I said. Which was at least truthful. I had some vague idea about turning up at his work and waiting outside to see if I could spot him. Maybe talk to him. Maybe not.

'Have you told John and Jackie?' asked Nell. She doesn't pull her punches, Nell, prosthetic hand or not.

'Not yet,' I admitted. I'd been debating with myself. Papa John and Jackie are great and everything, but fostering's their job. They can trade me in whenever they want and, once I've left them, whether that's at sixteen, eighteen or twenty-one, that's it. I need to find myself some long-term family. Someone who can't decide not to be related. So, despite wanting to ask Jackie's opinion, I'd decided to leave it – no point in *encouraging* them to get rid of me.

'Are you going to?' Honestly, why was Nell so on my case about this?

'And you tell your mum and dad everything, do you?'

She looked down. 'I didn't mean it like that.'

I missed Sasha. You could have a heated debate and she'd come right back at you, all guns blazing. Nell just crumpled.

'I haven't told them yet, OK? I'm not even sure there's anything to tell. That's all. No biggie.'

Nell nodded, still looking down.

'I don't want to hurt them. They've been brilliant. But what if they take it as a hint that I want to leave? I'll have to move again.'

'I get it,' said Nell. She lifted her head at last and looked at me. 'Are you going on your own then? All the way to Plymouth?'

I hadn't thought about it. I guess I was. I'd been with the girls before, but never on my own.

'I could come with you,' Nell offered. 'If you want.'

'Why would you want to traipse all the way to Plymouth, just to watch me maybe talk to my father?'

'Because, whatever you think is going to happen, it might go completely differently. And I might regret that I wasn't there for you. That's what friends do. Be there for each other. No matter what.'

Seemed a bit of overkill, to be honest, just for a trip to Plymouth. But the company would be good.

'Well, if you're sure,' I said.

'Positive.' Her face split into a grin. 'It'll be fun. A day out.'

'We could go shopping too,' I said. 'You know, after we've done the dad bit.'

'We could walk along the Hoe, have lunch by the sea.'

'I have lunch by the sea every day.'

'But not with views like those,' said Nell. 'You can't beat the Hoe for panoramic.'

She was right. You couldn't.

I was surprised that Nell would be allowed to go to Plymouth. Her mum didn't even like her coming down to the quay. 'What are you going to tell your mum?'

Nell nibbled her bottom lip. 'I've got the job at the deli. It's the perfect cover. Mum won't suspect a thing.' But she didn't sound all that convincing.

CHAPTER 11
SASHA

I used to think if you were totally immersed in cringe-factor ten all the time, you would get used to it. But it's not true. I'd spent nearly a week with Dad and Clarisse and the cringe hadn't lessened. Neither had my nauseated reaction to them. I mean, I know the French are more tactile, but there is a time and a place, people. And this was neither.

On Saturday morning, Dad announced that he wasn't going to work. We'd go out. Just the three of us.

Cue the internal sarky cheering. I couldn't think of anything better. Anything I'd like more. Honestly. It was my dream come true, right there.

'I thought we could catch the train along the lake to Montreux, then get the mountain train up to Gstaad.'

'What's at Gstaad?' I asked. It sounded like a lot of train.

'It's a beautiful ski resort,' said Dad.

I frowned. 'But it's August. And it's like forty degrees out. Surely they don't have snow?'

Dad laughed. Seriously. What was so funny?

'Of course there's no snow there now. But it's a beautiful area – the mountains are stunning.'

'What else?'

'Stunning mountains and wonderful scenery aren't enough?' asked Dad. He looked genuinely puzzled. 'Well, there's some chairlifts and cable cars in the area. Perhaps we could go up to the top of one of the mountains.'

'And what's there?' I asked. Seriously. What didn't he get? 'Let me guess. More scenery.'

Dad nodded, a bit deflated.

'So, there's literally nothing there?'

'I have heard,' said Clarisse, butting in, 'that there are some of the most gorgeous shops in the world in Gstaad.'

This time it was Dad's turn to look less enthusiastic.

I googled the shops in Gstaad. Clarisse was right. And they were freaking expensive.

'Perhaps we should do something more local,' said Dad, 'if you're not keen.'

'No,' I said quickly. 'I don't want to stop you from doing what you want to do. Shopping in Gstaad it is.'

With any luck, I'd be able to get some guilty-absent-father money off Dad, then lose them for the day.

We started out early. Pre-seven early. That was the first mistake. Every idiot knows that teens operate in a different time zone. But no. We had to make the 'best of the day' and this required me to leave my bed at dawn and walk down the road to the station. Going in Switzerland's favour was the absolute certainty that our train would arrive on time. Which it did. Also the guarantee it would be one of those swanky, state-of-the-art double-decker trains. Which it was.

I cheered up fractionally when I managed to obtain breakfast pastries and a strong coffee at the station for an excellent train picnic *and* I made them sit upstairs – like I said to Dad, if there are views, might as well be able to see them. The train followed the lake, sometimes skirting right along the edge, before veering off to higher ground.

The lake was sparkling as the sun rose higher over it. I tried my best not to look, as I thought if I paid too much attention to the scenery Dad would never let me hear the end of it. But he was too interested in Clarisse to care about me or the landscape.

We changed trains in Montreux, swapping the fast, sleek train for a smaller one.

'It's along this line that the language changes from French to German,' said Dad.

'Really?' I checked the list of stations and saw that the very French-sounding Rougemont was followed by a decidedly German-sounding Saanen. It must be so weird for the people living round there. Or maybe not. Perhaps they switched and swapped languages so easily that they barely noticed. I would have to watch out to see if the conductor changed languages when asking for tickets.

As the train travelled up and up from Montreux, much slower than the previous train, I realised that I had to be engrossed in the scenery, or in my phone, or else I was going to be totally grossed out by my father. He had Clarisse's hand in his and he was stroking it. Every now and then he would lean over and whisper something in her ear, and then she'd laugh, then he'd laugh.

'Want to share the joke?' I muttered.

'Sorry, *ma petite*?' said Dad.

'Never mind, I'm going for a walk.'

'On a train?' said Clarisse, and they both laughed.

I got up and walked down the train. At end of the last carriage, I looked out through the back window, seeing the track falling away as we carried on up the valley. What I'd considered to be mountains along the side of the lake were mere hills. These were mountains. I had to crane my neck to see the summits through the train windows. The air was cooler, fresher and it seemed that the greens were greener, like the whole place had been digitally remastered.

'Are you OK, *mademoiselle*?' asked the conductor.

'*Oui, merci,*' I replied. And I was. Now I was away from the lovebirds.

I hoped that they'd want to do their own thing for the day. I could get some money off Dad, arrange a time to meet back at the station and have the day to myself. I could mooch round the shops, try out the famous hot chocolate and perhaps get a chairlift if there was time.

'Oh, there you are.' Dad swayed his way down the carriage towards me.

'Hey,' I said.

'So? What do you think?' He nodded towards the views outside.

'You were right. This is amazing.'

He looked pleased. Now was my chance.

'Listen, Dad. I thought I'd go off by myself today. You know, have a bit of an explore, take in the sights, do the shops, give you and Clarisse a bit of space. If I could get a bit of cash, I'll be out of your hair for the day. Then I could meet you back at the station.'

'What? No way. The whole purpose of the day is for me to spend some time with you, and for you to get to know Clarisse a bit better.'

'Think I know all I need to.'

'What's that supposed to mean?'

'Nothing,' I said. Why couldn't I just do what I wanted?

'No. You're coming with us. End of.' He walked away down the carriage, leaving me gripping the seat beside me and gritting my teeth. I would make him regret that decision.

The train pulled into Gstaad as the station clock ticked over to the exact arrival time. It was clear the staff took a disproportionate amount of pleasure in punctuality. Dad and Clarisse got off the train and I followed.

'First stop: lunch,' Dad declared. 'We've got a choice. Either up the cable car and lunch on top of a mountain, or find a café in the town?'

Definitely in the town. Near the shops. 'Café in town,' I said.

'I think the cable car first. Then we can walk down afterwards,' said Clarisse over me.

'Oh, good idea.' Dad nodded. As if I had said nothing. Was I even here?

He led the way towards the chairlift station. Out of the building came a cluster of thick wires, which went steeply up, parallel to the mountain, with what looked like garden benches dangling from them. I gulped. It didn't look safe.

'Dad, I don't want to cramp your style. I'm fine staying in the town. I promise I'll be sensible. I'll just stay on the main street.' Anything but going on that contraption.

'Listen,' said Dad, 'I've said already, it's a day for us to be together.' And he walked off into the building, Clarisse by his side.

I gulped and followed.

Within minutes we were queuing up, waiting for our turn. I looked to see how the chairlifts worked. All the wires seemed solid. No fraying. That was hopeful. I was still worried, though. It didn't seem like a lot holding you up.

'Natasha,' said Dad, 'the chairs are for two people. You go first and Clarisse and I will be in the chair behind you.'

Should I tell him how scared I was? Then I

thought of home, and the gang, and Hetal's nani. No regrets. Try something new. Live a little. But also, possibly, die young in a chairlift accident.

When my turn came, I walked forward and stood on the footprints. The bench came sweeping round the end of the run, slowed down momentarily before it bumped into my legs, knocking me back into the seat, and then it picked up speed and whooshed me out of the building, over a massive drop and out over the hillside.

It was amazing! I yanked the metal frame down over my head, giving my feet something to rest on rather than dangling. It was so quiet. Only the whirring as I bumped over each pylon disturbed the silence. And then I realised it wasn't silent. There were birds singing in the trees below, the gushing of a mountain stream and, in the distance, the clang of Swiss cowbells.

I was starting to enjoy it when behind me I heard Clarisse laugh. I groaned. If a genie appeared now and gave me three wishes, I'd wish for Cam, Hetal and Nell. But there was no genie. I was stuck with that pair. As the chair approached the terminal building, I wondered if I ran quick enough whether I could lose them before their chair arrived.

'How was that?' asked Dad, as we stood outside

the station. I opened my mouth to reply when Clarisse butted in.

'*Formidable*! Thank you so much for bringing me here.'

Surely Dad would correct her? Say he was asking me.

'My pleasure,' he said. 'Delighted you enjoyed it.'

He linked his arm through hers and they walked off together up the short path towards the mountain-top restaurant, leaving me behind, fuming and wishing there was some way for me to escape. But Dad had the money and the tickets. There was nothing for it. I started walking after them, kicking stones out of the way, the exhilaration of the chairlift gone, leaving me with nothing but an empty feeling in my stomach.

CHAPTER 12
NELL

Things were going my way. Definitely. Which meant that surely there would be no problem about asking for a day off when I'd only been working there three days and she had a member of staff already on holiday. No problem at all with that.

Why had I offered to go with Cam? It would have been so much easier to let her go by herself. She might even have wanted to, if it wasn't for me and my big mouth not giving her the option. And now I had to somehow wangle a day off. Crapsicles.

I got to work just before seven. The day felt new, with the special sort of light you only get to see if you're up too early or out too late. I pushed open the shop door, the bell jangling.

'Morning, Nell,' said Wendy. 'How's things this

morning?' She was the most cheerful person I'd ever met. I wondered if it was just a front or was she genuinely that happy all the way through?

'OK.' I found my apron and pulled it on over my head. On my first morning I'd had to ask awkwardly whether Wendy would help tie it behind my back. And she had, without a flinch, or an overly sympathetic air. She'd just tied the strings, carrying on her conversation without missing a beat. When I'd thanked her, she'd waved it away with a 'no problem'. I wanted to carry her around with me and say to people, 'Look, *this* is how you should treat me.' The day after when I went to put it on, I found that my apron had been neatly adapted using Velcro, so that it could be fastened easily with one hand.

I washed my hands and put on plastic gloves. Then I set about arranging the sausage rolls that Wendy was crimping on a baking tray before pushing them into the oven. My stomach growled. The smell of this place was just so good. Wendy reckoned I'd get immune to it after a while but it hadn't happened yet. I still wanted to eat the displays.

Wendy turned up the radio and started singing. The shop didn't open till eight and the time before then was spent preparing, baking and singing.

'Come on, Nell, join in,' she said as she belted out the best of the 1980s hits.

There was no way I could sing in front of her.

'Before my time,' I replied. 'Sorry.'

'Well, if you work here long enough, you'll soon pick them up.' And she carried on singing.

There was part of me that regretted not joining in. It looked fun. But there was no way. I'd only mess it up.

'Wendy?' I said, as I went to turn the 'closed' sign to 'open'. I had to ask. I had no idea what I'd do if she said no. I didn't want to let Cam down. But I didn't want to let Wendy down either.

'Yes,' said Wendy.

'I was wondering if I could have Thursday off?'

Wendy frowned a bit. Not a lot. But a bit. And it made a pain in my insides.

'How come?' she asked. 'It's quite unusual to get time off in your first week, and you know Tom is away.'

I couldn't tell her about Cam. It wasn't my secret to tell. I'd have to make something up.

'My aunt died. It's her funeral.' My fingers were crossed tight behind my back. Would she believe me?

Wendy's face changed in an instant. 'Oh, honey flower, why didn't you say? Of course. I'm so sorry

to hear that. Take the day off.' And she turned back
to her baking.

The pain in my stomach didn't go away, and it
was with a funny feeling that I texted Cam later
that morning in between customers.

Me: *Thursday is on – got the day off.*
Cam: *Nice work. Me too.*

If this was living life with no regrets, why did it feel
so bad?

CHAPTER 13
HETAL

From the instant I woke up, I could feel it in my veins. This was no longer about a tiny star on an insignificant pedestal. This wasn't a little skirmish. This was war. I would make Finn eat his words. I would beat him all around science camp with my knowledge.

I jumped out of bed. Today was going to be the day I showed them all.

Mum had always said that it wasn't nice for girls to want to win. She'd always said that she lost every board game she played with my father, because it made him feel good. Dad laughed this off, claiming that he'd always won fair and square. And I was never sure who was telling the truth. Should I play it down maybe?

But the thought had gone as quickly as it had come. It was the twenty-first century, for goodness sake, and it shouldn't matter who wins, boy or girl. Just the best scientist. And that was me. I had read a study once that found girls have to do consistently better in order to achieve the same rewards as boys. I pushed the niggle to the back of my brain. I would simply have to be even better.

I went for a run round the circuit of the camp. It was still early and most people were still in bed. I couldn't sleep. My brain seemed to be wired awake. And studies show that physical activity boosts brain power. I wasn't too proud to make the most of every edge I could get.

I loaded up on berries and slow-release cereals at breakfast.

'What happened to the usual sugar-fuelled Hetal?' asked Maddy, glancing at my bowl of blueberries and porridge.

'She wants to win.' I smiled, like this was a light-hearted thing, but it was anything but. I would do more than win this. I would own it.

The first session was chemical engineering. I concentrated hard. It was one area I didn't feel too confident in. But I'd done some reading up on it the night before, so hopefully I was ahead of the pack.

After answering three questions in a row, on the fourth the leader said, 'How about giving someone else a chance, Hetal?'

I put my hand down, my face glowing. Had I pushed it too far? Was I turning into an annoying know-it-all? No one likes that. But what if I know the answer? Should I hold back to give someone else a turn? I sat still and didn't put my hand up again that session.

It felt as if someone had plunged my candle into a bucket of water. The confidence I'd felt earlier had evaporated. How could I feel like I could conquer the world one minute and the next minute feel like I wanted to curl up and die? I mean, I understand the brain chemistry a bit but, seriously, science doesn't prepare you for how that mix of chemicals feels. I wanted to go back to bed and pull the duvet over my head. It took all the strength I had to stay there. Finn was in all of my sessions and I watched as he answered question after question. Why wasn't anyone telling him to put his hand down?

At break, I grabbed some food and went off to sit by myself. Having not missed home for days, I now longed to be there. I pulled out my phone.

Me: *Hey guys. How's it going? I'm surviving
        science camp. Bit intense tbh.*

Nell: *Missing you – how long have you got left? Off
        with Cam tomorrow to Plymouth.*

Sasha: *Geneva's nice. Dad and gf, not so much. Bit
        like science camp – too intense!*

Cam: *What Nell's not telling you is that we're
        stalking my birth father.*

Me: *What? For real?*

Sasha: *That's major Cam – you're doing this right,
        aren't you? Like, you've told John and Jackie?*

Cam: *There might be nothing to tell.*

Sasha: *If you're going all the way to Plymouth to see
        him, there's something to tell.*

Me: *Good luck anyway with it, Cam.*

I waited and waited on my phone, but no more messages came. Sasha had probably said exactly what Cam was thinking but trying to ignore. Cam does that when she's being stubborn. You can tell her and tell her, but unless she wants to hear it, she won't.

Me: *What are you doing with yourself in Geneva
        then Sasha?*

I waited some more.

Me: *Did you get that job in the end, Nell?*

Still nothing. Great. I scrolled through the photos Sasha had posted, looking at the beautiful scenery, and her gorgeous selfies. I missed her. I missed Cam and her quick humour. I missed Nell. I missed us being together for the summer. In the distance I heard the bell ring for the next session. I checked my phone one last time for messages, tipped my drink into a bush and went to the next workshop.

I arrived a couple of minutes late and quietly pushed my way to the back of the lab. The tutor was already talking us through the experiment he'd prepared for us. I knew of the experiment, but had never done it myself.

'So,' said the tutor, 'any questions?'

There were a couple from the front, mainly about how to choose the best apparatus for the job, but once they had been answered, we were left to get on with it.

I was partnered with a tall boy. I was just pulling out the stands we would need when I heard Finn.

'You don't mind swapping, do you?' He was talking to the tall kid.

'No, sure thing.'

I turned. 'Did you want to check with me, if I minded swapping?'

'What? Did you want to work with Courtney?' said Finn, his eyes wide, pointing to the blonde girl he'd been partnered with.

I looked at her. She seemed to be smiling at the tall kid as if they were in on a joke. It made me feel awkward.

'Well, let's get started,' I said. 'We've already wasted a few minutes messing about swapping.'

'Yes, ma'am!' He saluted.

He weighed out the chemicals we needed, while I measured the sulphuric acid. Why had he swapped? Didn't he want to work with Courtney? Perhaps he was going to sabotage the experiment, making sure he got the right results and I didn't. But we were being marked as a team.

I looked at him sideways between the test tubes gripped in their stands. His face was lit by the flicker of a Bunsen burner, making his eyes sparkle. It didn't make sense. There was no logical explanation for it. And my brain didn't like unanswered questions. I was going to have to keep a very close eye on him. Finn was up to something.

CHAPTER 14
CAM

The three days till Thursday dragged like a snail on a go-slow. Before I looked at the clock, I'd try and guess how many minutes had passed since I'd last looked. I was always wrong. Why did time always slow down when you wanted it to speed up?

'What's up with you?' said Papa John on Tuesday. 'You seem a bit distracted this week.'

'Huh?'

'My point exactly.'

'Oh. It's nothing. Just thinking, that's all.'

Papa John disappeared into the back room, shaking his head and muttering.

I had to find a way to focus. I threw myself into anything that needed doing, sorting out stack after stack of products. Some had clearly been there a long time. Yellowing boxes and crispy sellotape told me that some ranges didn't have a high turnover of stock.

I started keeping a list of things that looked like they'd not been sold in a decade.

'Papa John,' I called, as he emerged from the back room on Wednesday. He came over.

'Look at this shelf. None of this stock has moved in ages.'

'How do you know?' he asked.

'Well, the products were spider-webbed to the shelf and, right at the back, I found an old mouse nest.'

Papa John nodded. 'OK.'

'I was thinking we could stick all the old stock into a discount bucket, just to shift it, then we could use this shelf to display that new range of power tools you were going on about.'

His eyebrows shot up then knitted back down as he thought.

'That's not a bad idea,' he said finally. 'Not bad at all. I was wondering where we were going to find the space to do those tools justice. Good job.'

Rummaging through the storeroom out back, I found a sturdy old wooden crate which I lugged through into the store. I swept all the old stock into it and cleaned the shelves down.

All I needed to do was accessorise it with an 'All items a pound' sign and I was done. I checked the clock. It was just about lunchtime. I grabbed my phone and skipped out. I only had an afternoon and a night until I would be going to Plymouth to meet him. My birth father. I took my sandwich down to the bench and sat munching.

How was I going to play it? What should I say? Would he believe me? Maybe he'd been looking for me, too, and he'd be excited to finally meet me. He'd hug me and tell me he had so much to tell me. Would Nell mind if we went off to have a coffee? I'm sure she wouldn't. It was to be expected really. You don't meet your daughter, have a two-minute chat, then say see you later. Perhaps coffee wouldn't be enough. Perhaps he'd take the afternoon off work. He might even give us a lift home in his car. I bet he has a really fancy car. I mean, he's really high up in the company he works at, so he must.

The afternoon seemed to go more quickly, as I mentally listed the things I had to tell him. He'd want to know all about John and Jackie, of course, and school. Wouldn't it be weird if I had similar interests to him?

Every now and again, a little warning would sound in my head. But I ignored it. Negative thinking wouldn't help. I had to go into this with a positive attitude. Believe and it will happen, don't they say?

By the end of the day, the newly cleaned shelves were stocked with the smart new range of power tools.

'Wow, Cam, that's looking fantastic. You've certainly earned your day off.'

'Thanks,' I said, grinning.

'And Cam? I'm proud of you – great job.'

I kept smiling, but my heart fell a little bit. My birth father was going to have a lot to live up to. But Papa John wouldn't be there forever. I needed to think long term.

CHAPTER 15
SASHA

Dad had already left for work, leaving me in with Clarisse. Yeah. Cue massive cheering from me. Not. I had just poured myself a large black coffee from the pot when Clarisse appeared, looking all chic and sexy. How did she do that this early in the morning? When I got up I always had dried drool on my face and my hair stuck out at odd angles.

I ignored her and tapped on my phone, while sipping my coffee. We didn't need air conditioning in here. The atmosphere was already pretty icy.

'What are you doing today?' Clarisse asked in her thick French accent.

I shrugged. I hadn't given it much thought.

'I'm going into Geneva. Clothes shopping.'

Despite myself, my ears pricked up.

'And I was wondering if you wanted to come too?'

Clothes shopping. In Geneva. One of the fashion centres of the world. With someone who, despite all her many and obvious faults, had exquisite taste in clothes. I'd just have to put up with, you know, her.

'Your dad said that you needed something better to wear.'

I'm sorry, what now? What was wrong with the clothes I had? I couldn't believe it: this was a makeover trip!

'Are you sure you want to risk being seen with me? You know, looking like this?' I didn't know if sarcasm translated, and I didn't care.

'Well, we'll get you something early on, then you can wear your new clothes while we shop for more.' Clearly no, it didn't.

'Look, if I wanted to hook myself a bloke who was massively older than me, then I'd be right there with you but, thanks, think I'll stick around here for the day.'

Clarisse's red lips squashed themselves into a thin line. 'Suit yourself.' Picking up her handbag and sunglasses, she slammed the door as she left.

The low-level annoyance that had been

simmering away for the last week or so threatened to engulf me. But there was no way, *no way*, I was going to let *her* ruin my day. She was gone. Dad was out. I had a day to do what I liked. With whoever I liked. A shiver of excitement pulsed over my skin. Perhaps a drink at the local café to start with? I tipped my coffee away, picked up my sunglasses and left.

As I got to the café, I scanned around. Was he working today? Pierre had promised me that he'd walk me along the lakeside and I was all set to cash in that promise. I spotted him, working behind the bar, making coffees. I could smell the freshly ground beans.

I walked slowly past the bar. I knew I looked good. Despite what Dad and Clarisse thought, these shorts did wonders for me. I sat down in my usual shady spot and watched Pierre as he delivered a tray of drinks to a couple on the other side of the restaurant. He tucked the tray under his arm and headed straight towards me.

'Good morning, *mademoiselle*,' he said, his smile liquefying my insides.

'Hi,' I said.

'What can I get for you?'

I bit my bottom lip. Did I have the nerve to say it?

'How about that lakeside walk you promised? And I'll get a mocha while I'm waiting.'

He grinned. 'One mocha coming right up.'

I watched him go back over to the bar. He made a mocha while talking to the other waiter. They both laughed and I tried hard not to imagine they were laughing at me.

He came back over, carrying the steaming cup. 'One mocha, *mademoiselle*. And I am happy to say that I can finish work in half an hour. So I am at your disposal.'

Despite wanting to whoop and punch the air, I held it together. I am a sophisticated woman, who knows what she wants and gets it. I smiled. 'See you at the water's edge in an hour then?'

'It's a date.' He leaned forward to kiss my hand. 'And perhaps bring your swimming stuff. We could hire a boat and go out on the lake, if you liked.'

As I sipped my coffee, my hand fizzed and tingled where his lips had touched my skin. This was going to be a good day.

An hour later I strolled down to the lake, beach bag slung over one shoulder and an excited buzz in my head. Pierre was already there. I waved, then remembered I was supposed to be playing it cool.

But he didn't seem to worry as he waved back. He looked younger, somehow, out of his waiter's uniform.

'Hello,' he said, kissing me on both cheeks, my skin on fire where his lips touched. I'd seen kids in town kissing each other in greeting, but I couldn't get used to it. It felt so ... weird. Over-familiar somehow. But I wasn't about to complain.

'I've got us a boat.' He nodded towards a small sailing boat, bobbing and pulling at her mooring. He held my hand as we clambered aboard. The swell rocking the boat felt familiar under my feet.

'Have you sailed before?' he asked.

Dropping my bag onto the deck, I hopped ashore, slackened off the rope and, looping it over, jumped back on board, giving the boat a push off as I did so.

'Once or twice,' I said.

Pierre grinned and started to raise the sail. It felt good to be doing something. For days I'd done nothing but sit around and making my blood pump and getting out of breath felt fabulous. Though I'm not sure that was all down to the physical effort of getting the sailing boat to the middle of the lake. It wasn't a big boat and Pierre and I kept touching, fingers reaching for the same ropes, feet searching for the same footholds. We didn't talk much, just worked together to get the boat to where we wanted it, out of the path of the large ferries zigzagging the lake. Away from other people.

'How about here?' I said, looking around. The nearest boats were the size of toys and the shoreline was away in the distance.

Pierre nodded and flicked his hair out of his eyes. I had my bikini on under my clothes, so stepped out of my shorts and pulled off my T-shirt.

'Come on, what are you waiting for?' I crowed. I stood on the nose of the boat and dived in. The cold water took my breath away. But it was gorgeous. Deliciously refreshing. I surfaced and pushed back my hair. Pierre was standing on the edge of the boat.

'The water's lovely,' was what I was trying to say, when Pierre landed near me and deluged me in an enormous splash of water. He'd done that on purpose. I dived and found his feet. Grabbing them, I dunked him. He thrashed about a bit before surfacing, coughing and spitting water.

'You little devil.' He ducked to get my feet. I screamed and pulled away, swimming round the boat. I heard him come up for air.

'Missed me,' I shouted. I heard him laugh and swear. I laughed too.

After we'd swum till my arms ached, we pulled ourselves back into the boat, and just lay there, dripping, the heat of the sun quickly warming my body and drying my skin.

'That was fun,' I said.

'It was,' nodded Pierre. 'You are one special girl.'

His eyes were looking at me, and against the blue of the water and the blue of the sky, they looked extra dark. I leaned over and kissed him. Gently at first then less so as I got into it. Surrounded by lake and mountains and water and gorgeous boy, I was swept away by a different sort of tide. As Pierre kissed back, his arms pulling me closer, I thought briefly that this really was a summer of no regrets.

CHAPTER 16
NELL

I'd prepared well. I had to cover all my bases. Mum thought I was working. Dad thought I was working. I'd told Cam not to tell her dad she was going with me, just in case Mum popped into the hardware shop. Wendy thought I was at my aunt's funeral. I'd covered all eventualities. But my insides still felt in a knot. I'd woken up with a jolt the night before, panicking that everyone had found out. It had taken me ages to get back to sleep.

I set off for the bus stop near Cam's house at the usual time for work and then hung about for ages. By the time she got there my lack of sleep was seriously catching up with me.

'You looked wrecked,' said Cam as she approached.

'Thanks, I am,' I stifled a yawn. We caught the bus heading to Plymouth. I tried to stay awake but my head kept dropping forwards, then sideways.

'Didn't you sleep very well?'

'Not really.'

'Sign of a guilty conscience,' said Cam, grinning.

What did she mean by that? I'm not guilty of doing anything wrong. Well, not really wrong. Just a few white lies here and there. I must have looked worried as Cam jabbed me in the ribs with her elbow.

'Only kidding. Lighten up, will you? I'm the one supposed to be stressed out today, not you.'

She was right. I was so wrapped up in my problems that I hadn't given what she was going through a second thought. What a totally crap friend I was.

'Sorry, Cam, I didn't think.'

She laughed, throwing her pink head back, getting a ton of frowns from the people around us.

'Kidding again, Nell. Look. We've got a day to ourselves. A day off work. Let's just enjoy ourselves, OK? No regrets?'

I smiled. Cam was right. I needed to lighten up. I didn't want to ruin her day off.

She linked her arm through mine. 'What shall we do first? The Hoe? Shops? Snack?'

'I reckon we should check out where your father works first,' I said. 'That is the reason we're going, isn't it?'

'Killjoy.' She pulled out a piece of paper. She'd written the address down, and had ringed the postcode. We worked out how far it was from the bus terminal. Not far. So we could do lots of what we planned and still stalk Cam's birth father.

As we pulled into the station, Cam dragged me off the bus, pushing everyone out of our way, getting more frowns from the other passengers. It was like she didn't even notice. Did she care? I apologised as I was pulled past person after person.

'OK, coffee, then shopping, then father hunting. Then this afternoon, the Hoe. And we'll get home in time for tea.'

It wasn't a question. It was what was going to happen. Cam was like that. Decisive. And I was glad. Making decisions brings me out in a rash.

It was nearly lunchtime when, laden with bags of bargains, the upside of having jobs and disposable income (well, Cam had subbed me till my first pay day, but I'm going to pay her back the instant I get paid), we decided to go and wait outside Cam's father's workplace.

'You decided what you're going to say?' I asked. She'd been quite quiet for the last few minutes.

'I guess, just the obvious.' She shrugged. 'There's no other way, is there?'

'I guess not.'

We sat down on a bench. The day was turning out to be a warm one, not overpoweringly hot, just nice, so we sat in the sun, opposite the main rotating doors.

At first only a few people came out but, as it got closer to lunchtime, more and more were pouring out the doors.

'Can you see him?' asked Cam. Her eyes were darting everywhere, trying to check everyone's face.

'No, not yet,' I was searching but, honestly, I wasn't sure I would recognise him. I was basically looking for someone who looked like Cam. Only without the pink hair.

'There,' said Cam suddenly. She pointed.

A man in a pinstriped suit was striding away across the pedestrianised area and towards the city centre.

'Come on.'

She jumped up, and I followed. She was nearly

running. We must've looked so odd, running after some suited man. What would people think? I stopped and let Cam carry on. It was her father. I was only here for support. And to carry the shopping.

I watched as Cam ran to her father and tapped him on the shoulder. He stopped and turned round. He looked so like her. There wasn't any doubt that it was him. She started talking to him.

I walked back to the bench and sat down, heaving the shopping bags up beside me so they didn't get dirty. I'd just wait here till they were done.

CHAPTER 17
HETAL

Finn plonked his tray down next to me at lunch. 'This seat taken?'

I looked around me at all the empty seats. Seriously? And this guy was supposed to be clever. 'No. Clearly.'

He sat down and started to eat his pasta bake. I wondered why he wasn't sitting with his friends. They were chatting noisily at a table on the other side of the dining hall.

I carried on eating, stabbing a cherry tomato with my fork.

'So? How are you finding it?'

He was trying to talk to me? I narrowed my eyes a bit, trying to think why he'd bother.

'It's alright.'

'I haven't told any of my mates back home that I'm here,' he said, still eating. 'They'd think I was a massive loser.'

Why was he talking? Why was he telling me this?

'Oh.' Hopefully he'd take the hint and get lost.

'But I've been thinking – does that make me a massive loser for not being able to tell them about it?'

Honestly, this was all a bit heavy for me.

'It's alright for you,' he said. 'You're rocking the geek chic look.'

I looked at him properly now. It sounded like there was a compliment buried in there somewhere.

'You think it's easy for me to be here?'

'Sure,' he said.

'Anyone told you today to stop answering questions and give someone else a chance?'

He stopped. Fork in mid-air. Mouth slightly open.

'Anyone told you that people don't like smart girls? That you should stop trying so hard? That no one will want you if you're cleverer than them?'

He was looking genuinely shocked.

'Didn't think so. If you'll excuse me, I think I've had all I can stomach.' I picked up my tray, scrapped my lunch into the bin and walked out of the dining hall.

The instant the fresh air hit my face, my bones

turned to jelly. What had gotten into me? I never act like that. I folded my arms around myself to try and get them to stop shaking. I hated confrontation. I walked fast along the path. I needed to hide under my duvet for a bit.

As I was turning the corner to my cabin, Finn came skidding up behind me.

'Hetal, wait.'

The temptation to rush inside and shut the door was overwhelming.

'Wait!'

I turned round, my arms still folded tight.

He stopped in front of me. He was taller than me and, this close up, I could see how blue his eyes were. He was breathing fast.

'Look, Hetal. I'm sorry. I didn't mean to upset you.' He pulled his hand through his hair. 'Crap. That was the last thing I wanted to do.'

My insides were churning.

'It's OK,' I said. 'Perhaps I shouldn't have said all that stuff.'

'You totally should. I didn't think.'

'Look, if you're trying to be nice so I stop beating you in the daily awards…'

Finn laughed. 'There's not a chance of that, is there? OK, you're on. I'll stop holding back.'

'Oh funny! You're all in, just like me,' I said, calling his bluff.

He grinned. 'That trophy's got my name all over it.'

'That sounds like fighting talk,' I put on an American accent.

Finn just smiled. 'May the best scientist win.' He held out his hand.

Bit old-fashioned, but I took it and shook it firmly. His hand felt soft and warm and strong. I might have held onto it for a fraction of a second too long. Like 0.0001 of a second.

That afternoon, I was back. It was like the morning, only with a warm glow. I still wanted to beat Finn, but not in an annihilation sense anymore. We were in the same classes, and it was a race to see who could get their hands up the fastest. I think the others were noticing, as there were ripples of giggles at every question.

That evening, after being enthralled by Dr Angela, Maddy and I wandered along the paths, slowly making our way to dinner.

'I reckon Finn likes you,' said Maddy.

'What? No way.'

'He came to sit next to you at lunch, didn't he?'

'Only to insult me.'

'Really? I reckon he was trying to chat you up.'

'Well, it backfired,' I said.

Maddy laughed. 'So what's with the answering questions thing?'

'It's not a thing.' I struggled to explain. 'It's just...' What was it exactly? 'It's just friendly competition.'

Maddy laughed again. 'I've never heard it called that before.'

I changed the subject and then zoned out as Maddy rambled on. Could she be right? Could Finn see me like that? And what if he did? I didn't feel the same way. Did I?

We got our food and went to sit at the table nearest the door. It was still warm and the breeze drifting in was nice. I saw Finn and a couple of his friends line up to get their food. He caught my eye. I saw him notice the empty seat next to me. He started heading my way, when a girl from the biochemistry session plonked her tray down next to me. He looked disappointed, then turned and went with his mates to another table.

I tried not to think about what Maddy had said.

At the end of the meal, Josh stood up and cleared his throat, waiting until we were all quiet.

'Now we do try to vary who wins the daily

trophy for effort and achievement, but the stories I've been hearing today from all the staff mean I have no choice.'

He was going to give it to Finn again.

'Could Finn Gilbertson come up, please?'

I surprised myself by feeling pleased for him. I'd got the trophy with me, ready to hand over.

'And could Hetal Badesha also come up, please?'

I walked to the front, smiling at Finn, holding out the trophy.

'Hang on there, Hetal,' said Josh, grinning. He put his arms over our shoulders, holding us on either side of him. 'It seems we have a bit of good old-fashioned camp rivalry going on here. And, today, because the staff couldn't pick between you, the unprecedented decision was made to award the trophy jointly. Congratulations, Finn and Hetal. I'm looking forward to seeing how this competition plays out.'

The dining hall clapped. We were both getting it? I beamed at Finn, who grinned back.

'You keep the trophy,' he said.

'No, you better had,' I said. 'Cos you're not going to be winning it again.'

Finn took it off me and winked.

Walking back to my table, I tried to tell myself

that I was bright and intelligent and immune from needing approval from others. But that wink had melted my insides and I'd never felt so amazing.

CHAPTER 18
CAM

Standing there, looking into a face which must be my father's, kind of took my breath away. They say you don't notice family similarities yourself, but I guess it's different if you've not seen your family before. He had wrinkles round his eyes and his hair was more receded than in his picture online, but it was him. No doubt. We had the same nose.

'Can I help you?' he asked, frowning a little.

'Um,' I said. I swear I'd got a whole speech prepared. I was planning to sound like the kind of daughter a person would be happy to hear about. The kind of daughter you would lift up and spin around.

He glanced at his watch and started to walk off.

'No wait!' This was my big chance. I mustn't blow it.

He stopped and looked at me again, his eyes flicking up to my pink hair. I should have worn a hat.

'Look, you see, the thing is. It's like this…'

'Could you get to the point? Are you homeless? Do you want money?'

What? Money? Homeless? 'No,' I said. 'That's not it.'

He looked at his watch again and frowned.

I took a deep breath. 'My name is Camille Morse. I'm sixteen and I think you are my biological father.'

His face drained, like someone had pulled the plug on his blood.

'No. There's no way.' His voice cracked.

'Did you know Lisa Morse? She, um, was into drugs? She was in Exeter that summer.'

He was shaking his head, like he wasn't really listening to me.

'She said you were my father.'

'Whatever she's told you, she's lying. Tell her to stop spreading stuff like that.'

'I can't.'

'Why not?' He'd raised his voice a bit.

'Cos she's dead.' I'd had to tell lots of people through my life. With time it'd got easier, I guess.

But the look of sympathy I get is pretty much uniform. It's a heartless sod who doesn't pity someone whose mum's dead.

'Dead?' He wasn't looking so great. He'd gone super-pale and was sweating along his top lip.

'Are you OK?' I asked. I didn't need the irony of finding my father only to have him keel over with a heart attack.

'Don't contact me again. Do you hear? Never again.'

He walked off through the crowds and, within seconds, I couldn't see him anymore. He was gone.

I couldn't move. My body had been hollowed out. I was just a shell, like an Easter egg.

Had that really happened? I'd met my dad and within minutes been told to never contact him again. He couldn't have meant it. Who would be that cold?

I turned around and walked towards the bench and Nell. But it was like I was looking at the world through a lens: everything seemed far away, nothing felt real. Nell came over and was talking to me, but I couldn't make out what she was saying. There was this buzzing in my head. 'Don't contact me again' kept ringing in my ears.

'Cam? Cam?' Nell held my face in her hands. Her

real hand was much warmer than her other one. 'Look, come and sit down. You don't have to talk.'

She led me over to the bench, where I perched on the edge. Why didn't he want to see me again? Didn't he want to know about me? Double-check that what I was saying was true? It didn't make any sense.

Nell rubbed her hand over my back and muttered about it all being OK. It wasn't all OK, but it felt good to have her there. She disappeared for a minute and returned with a cup of hot sweet tea.

'Drink this. You've had a shock.'

My head still felt like it was in a drum, but I took the tea off her anyway and took a sip. It was burning hot and tasted as if it had at least a dozen sugars.

'Flipping heck, Nell, how much sugar did you put in this?'

'My hand may have slipped,' she said. She was looking scared, the concern etched into her face.

'Thanks.' I took another sip. We sat there for a while, not talking.

The echoes of the conversation played over and over in my mind. Should I have told him differently? If I'd given him a chance to get used to the idea maybe? But who talks to a person like that? Who treats their own child like that?

Seriously, what a moron. He didn't even have the decency to say sorry about Mum being dead. Or ask if I'd travelled far. For all he knew, I could have travelled from Timbuktu. Well, I was better off without him, that's for sure. Who needs a tosser like that for a dad?

'How you doing?' asked Nell. I'd drunk half my tea and was feeling a bit more human. Less head in a box.

'Better. In fact, great. I feel great.' It was his loss. He'd had the opportunity to get to know his daughter and he'd blown it. I hoped that the knowledge would eat him up.

'Are you sure? Because you don't look so great.'

'Cheers,' I said.

'Sorry. Do you want to talk about it? I mean, you don't have to if you don't want to. I don't want to interfere.'

I love Nell, but she doesn't half witter.

'He doesn't want me to contact him again. He says he isn't my dad,' I said. I could feel the words catching in my throat, but I wasn't going to cry. Not in the centre of Plymouth. On a bench.

Nell handed me a tissue. 'I mean, did he even look at you? You're his total spit.'

I blew my nose. 'I don't know. He just seemed to

panic and then he told me never to contact him again and ran off.'

'I guess it might have come as quite a shock,' she said.

'You think he might not have known anything about me?'

'It's possible. And, even so, it was a long time ago, and I suppose he might not have been expecting to meet his daughter on his lunch break.'

I didn't want to admit it, but she could be right.

'Do you mind if we go home? Don't think I can face walking along the Hoe today.'

'No problem,' said Nell. 'We can do that another time. Come on. Let's go and catch the bus. Having to carry all these bags would have been a real nuisance anyway.'

She stood up and pulled me to my feet and shepherded me through the crowds to the bus terminal. I couldn't get my head round having seen my real father. He'd been right there in front of me. I could see his eyes, the same colour as mine, his hair the same colour as mine (under the pink). I'd ruined the one chance I'd have at getting to know him. To ask him some questions. To find out what he was like. Not in a fairy tale, spin you round when you first meet type way, but in a friendly, open, adult way.

Nell put me onto the right bus and sat me down nearest the window before squeezing herself and the shopping in after.

'OK?' she said.

I nodded and turned to look out of the window. It had started to rain, big fat drops hitting the glass and running down the window. As the bus drove through the streets, the outside world blurred. Nell fell asleep just outside Plymouth and her head rested gently on my shoulder.

This was my family now. In a few years, maybe sooner, John and Jackie would no longer be my foster-parents. I'd have to move out. Stand on my own two feet. And who would be there for me? My friends, that's who. My friends and no one else.

The thought made me feel sick. Everyone else had a family to look out for them. And not just parents. A whole team of people on their side – grandparents, aunts, uncles, cousins. Why had the universe decided that I didn't deserve that? And the one person who could have perhaps had a passing interest didn't want to know. The windows were steaming up as soaked people got onto the bus and the rain continued to hammer down. I couldn't reach the tissue Nell had given me without disturbing her, so I let the tears drip off my chin.

CHAPTER 19
SASHA

Pierre: *I have the evening off – fancy meeting up for a*
moonlit swim?

I can say, hand on heart, that this was the single most exciting text I had ever received. Maybe will ever receive.

Me: *Sure. See you by the lake at sunset.*

I pondered adding a kiss. He hadn't. Perhaps it was implied. I decided against it and pressed send, my palms sweating.

'Dad,' I shouted from the sofa. 'I'm out this evening, OK?'

He didn't need the details. I could make up

something about having to call home and needing a bit of privacy.

'Sorry, *ma cherie*,' he called back, 'it can't be tonight. We have dinner reservations.'

'Well, go without me. I'll be happy with takeout pizza.'

I was starting to feel panicky. I had to meet Pierre this evening. I could 100 per cent guarantee it would be one of my biggest life regrets if I didn't.

'There's nowhere that does takeout pizza.'

'Just you and Clarisse go. I'm more than happy staying in. I'll grab something here.'

Please. Please.

'Not this evening, Natasha. Any other evening, but not tonight. It's important.'

What could be so freaking important?

'Dad, please.' I was now actually begging. 'Please, could we move it to another night maybe?' Anything. I would do anything.

Dad came stomping out of his room, half-dressed, his shirt untucked and his hair messed up. 'Natasha! Enough. This restaurant has a waiting list weeks long. I have said you are coming and that is final.' He stormed back into his room and shut the door. I could hear him complaining about stubborn teenage daughters in French.

I texted Pierre: *Sorry, I can't make it tonight. Got to have dinner with my dad and his stupid girlfriend.*

Pierre: *Another time perhaps.*

My inner rage shifted up a gear from simmering. I was missing out on an awesome night to remember in order to spend the evening with Dad and Clarisse in some stupid posh restaurant. The unfairness made me mad. Like kick-a-wall mad. Like scream-and-shout mad.

It was a moonlit evening, perfect for lake swimming. Dad had dressed up in his cream linen suit and Clarisse was wearing an off-the-shoulder dress. Dad had suggested (from a safe distance) that I might like to dress the part too. I wore my super-short, cut-off, fraying jeans and a top which had the slogan 'YOLO' across the front. Dad said nothing, though Clarisse rolled her eyes when she saw me. She glared at my dad. Clearly I wasn't the only one who thought this evening's meal should be a romantic meal for the two of them.

Once we were seated, and the waiter had poured our drinks, Dad raised his glass. 'To my girls, what would I do without you both?' He repeated it in French for Clarisse, while I got over the wave of nausea. I was Dad's girl, true. And in some ways Clarisse was too – she was certainly young enough. But I was a daughter girl and she was girlfriend girl. Two totally different things. Hence the high reading on the barf-o-meter.

'It's so lovely being here, with you both. Thank you for both agreeing to come here this summer. It's made me very happy.' I suspected that Dad had already had a drink back at the apartment. He's usually more open with his feelings than most people I know, but this was bordering on the embarrassing, even for him.

The starters arrived and fortunately he was sidetracked by his mozzarella and tomato. I tucked into my tagliatelle, wishing the meal would hurry up and be over. Maybe if I was quick, there might still be time for a swim.

'Darling, you've got to try this,' said Dad, offering a forkful of mozzarella to Clarisse. She opened her mouth and he fed her.

I felt desperate. I needed to be anywhere, look anywhere, but at them. I became transfixed with the lights along the opposite shoreline of the lake. They must be a train as they were in a line and travelling quickly. I wished I was on that train, heading anywhere as long it was away from here.

By the time our main course arrived, I'd seen four trains travel along the shore, several small boats had sailed past on the lake and, seven times, Dad had muttered something into Clarisse's ear making her laugh. I just had to survive this cringe-fest, then I could escape back to the apartment. Perhaps I could say I was full, and didn't need dessert? Maybe I could have a headache? I searched for the perfect excuse.

I rammed mouthful after mouthful down. I wanted to leave, but I was still hungry. I'd eat as fast as I could, then I'd be off. I'm sure they wouldn't mind me leaving. Clarisse didn't want me there anyway. She kept looking at my clothes and frowning. I felt like smiling sweetly at her and saying I picked them just for her, because I know how much she likes the dress-down look.

I popped the last mouthful in and was about to speak when Dad beat me to it.

'Natasha, Clarisse and I have an announcement to make.'

How I swallowed that last mouthful, I will never know. Perhaps he was going to say that his contract had ended and that I'd have to go home early. But that's not something you get dressed up to say, is it?

'We are engaged,' said Dad. 'Clarisse has accepted my offer of marriage.'

'I'm going to be your step-mum,' added Clarisse.

They were both looking at me, eyes all wide and expectant.

Seriously? They were expecting me to be *happy* about this? Or perhaps they were telling me in a public place so I wouldn't make a scene.

'When did this happen?' I asked.

'On our day out to Gstaad,' said Dad.

'It was such a perfect day,' added Clarisse, smiling at Dad.

They'd got engaged while I was there? What was *wrong* with them? The world was going mad.

'I've got to go.' I stood up, scraping my chair, and ran out of the restaurant. I stopped halfway up the hill to throw up in a bin. Note to self: emotional upheaval on a full stomach plus running is not good for me. I leaned on the wall and wiped my mouth.

I didn't want to be on my own. It wasn't that late. I texted Pierre but didn't wait for the reply. I ran up to the apartment, washed my face, grabbed my costume and dashed out again, back down to the lake. Maybe he would be there already. I didn't know where he lived.

I stopped when I got to the waterfront, which was lit by short lamps along the water's edge. There were a few people walking along, enjoying the warm summer's evening. I scanned faces, looking for Pierre's.

I heard a laugh behind me. I spun round and looked out across the dark lake. Two heads were silhouetted, bobbing in the water. The laugh came from a girl. A high-pitched, flirty laugh.

'Oh, Pierre, you are funny.'

'And you are one special girl.' The heads merged together into one blob.

My head felt like it was going to blow up. That was supposed to be my evening. I was supposed to be the one in the lake. Not her. How could he have done that? He must have asked someone else the minute I said I couldn't make it.

How could I have been so *stupid*? Why had I allowed myself to fall for his lines? How naïve was I to have believed him when he said I was special?

Hot tears ran down my face. I hated Pierre. Hated my dad and stupid Clarisse. As I turned from the kissing heads, I spotted two piles of clothes on a low wall. I kicked them off the wall into the water. They drifted silently, blooming out across the surface of the water.

I definitely didn't want them to see me. I ran back to the apartment block. I leaned on the wall next to the entrance to catch my breath. I couldn't get the image of their heads pushed together out of my mind. Everywhere I looked, people were in love. Why couldn't Dad have waited till I wasn't around? Why did Clarisse have to be here at all? It was supposed to be my summer with Dad, not as a third wheel on their love wagon. Every time I thought about Pierre I felt embarrassed and angry. Stupid Sasha. Falling for the biggest cliché of all time – a handsome waiter on holiday. How could I have ever thought he'd be seriously interested in me?

I had to get out of there. I couldn't stand it anymore. Dad and Clarisse would get home and be all lovey-dovey on the sofa, and I'd have to spend the rest of the evening in my room. They wouldn't even notice I wasn't around.

I knew what I had to do.

I ran up the stairs, two at a time. I would have to be quick. I couldn't rely on them staying for dessert. I rammed everything into my suitcase, found my passport and rummaged in my emergency supplies from Mum. A credit card. For just in case, she'd said. Grabbing my phone and the charger, I pulled my bag out of my room. I stuck a note to my door. It said:

Sorry for leaving you so suddenly, I had a real bad headache. Don't disturb me – I'll be fine in the morning once I've slept it off. Sx

That should buy me some time. I wheeled my case out of the flat. As I was locking the door, the lift pinged to say it had arrived at our floor. Quickly I dragged my stuff into the stairwell and flattened myself against the wall. I was breathing hard and my hands were shaking, but I mustn't be seen, mustn't be heard.

The lift opened and Dad and Clarisse stepped out. Clarisse was giggling.

'It's a shame we couldn't stay for coffee,' she said. Yes, they should have done.

'I just wanted to check that Natasha's OK.'

'You worry about her too much. She's sixteen. Old enough to take care of herself.'

For the first time, I actually agreed with her. I was old enough to take care of myself. I waited till the apartment door closed before heaving my stuff down the stairs. I was going home.

I trundled my case down the road to the train station, bought a ticket to the airport and waited. When the train pulled in ten minutes later, I looked back up the hillside to the apartment block one last time. I could see Dad and Clarisse silhouetted on the balcony. It looked like they were kissing. I turned away. I'd had enough of watching other people kiss.

The airport was quieter than before, and there were very few desks open for check-in. I walked up to the first one I saw and asked how I could buy a ticket to the UK. The woman pointed to a different desk with a tired-looking man. Pulling my case behind me, I went over. In my very best French, I asked if I could buy a ticket.

'When for?'

'As soon as possible. I would like to leave tonight.'

'Ah, there are no more flights today.'

'What about first thing tomorrow?' I'd have to spend the night in the airport.

'There's not one till 1pm tomorrow.'

'That'll do.'

The man looked at me hard. 'Very well then.'

Within fifteen minutes, I had bought a ticket, been told where to check in from 10.30 the next morning and had loaded myself up with consolation snacks and a coffee. I found a bench in the busiest part of the airport and sat down, tucking my case under my feet. That way if I fell asleep, I'd feel it if someone tried to nick my case.

I sipped my coffee and tried to calm down. My hands hadn't stopped shaking since I'd left the restaurant. This summer was supposed to be the best, the summer of living without regrets, so why did it feel so rubbish? Here I was, sitting in an airport, alone. I'd run away from my dad. My holiday romance had dropped off a cliff. My friends didn't know what I was doing. My mum certainly didn't – she'd have hit the roof. If this was life with no regrets, why couldn't I tell people how I felt?

The coffee was good. I kept drinking it.

Did I feel embarrassed? I'd decided to come to Geneva for the summer and it had been a nightmare from start to finish. Was I ashamed to tell them I'd made the wrong call? Oh, the irony, I thought, as I sipped more coffee. I would have been better off staying at home for the summer like I'd planned.

I pulled out my phone, deleted Pierre's number and turned it off.

Finally. Something I wouldn't regret doing.

CHAPTER 20
NELL

I'd never seen Cam like that before. She was walking like a zombie, not really listening to what I was saying. I was totally panicking inside. I didn't want to be the one in charge of getting us home. I was sure to mess it up. When the bus pulled up at our stop, it was chucking it down but I didn't care. I was just pleased to be there. I pulled Cam along the aisle and down the steps. The rain soaked me instantly.

'Come on,' I said to her, 'let's get you home.'

I walked her as fast as I could until I got to her house. What was I going to tell her parents? It wasn't my place to tell and, as much as I lied to my parents, I didn't really want to start lying to other people's.

Jackie met us at the door. 'Oh, come in quickly,

you're both soaked through. Good shopping trip, I see?'

I looked at her, a bit confused. Then I remembered the bags I was carrying.

'Ah, yes. Very good, thank you.' I put down Cam's bags and glanced at her. She was still pale, her pink hair limp and dripping down her neck.

'I don't think Cam's feeling very well,' I said to Jackie. Cam didn't say anything. It was like she was still back in Plymouth.

'Love, are you alright?' The concern in Jackie's voice made my stomach stop churning. Cam would be OK with Jackie looking after her.

'I'd better be going,' I said.

'You don't want to dry off and wait for the rain to stop maybe?' asked Jackie.

'No, thanks. My mum will wonder where I am. See you later, Cam.'

Cam slowly turned to me, like she'd only just noticed I was there.

I pulled the front door shut behind me and walked along the road. I was already wet through, and I didn't mind the rain too much. Especially not in the summer when it wasn't icy cold.

I wondered what the time was. Because we'd come back earlier than planned, it fitted in with my work hours. No need to add extra lies to say why I was late home.

I pulled my phone out, shielding it from the worst of the rain. That's odd. I'd missed three calls from Mum. I stopped, my body suddenly cold.

It could be nothing. She knows I can't answer my phone while I'm at work. Bet she was ringing to ask me to pick up something on the way home. It was just my guilty conscience making me jumpy, that's all.

I started moving again, only faster this time. I'd hide my shopping in the shed like I'd planned. It'd be all good. I shot down the side passage of our house and stuffed the bags through the shed door and went back round to the front door.

As I started to unlock the door, it was pulled open.

'Nell! I've been worried sick.'

Mum filled the doorway, her face bright red and her hair pulled up into tufts.

'Hello to you too,' I said, dripping on the doorstep.

'Don't you give me cheek, young lady. I've been so worried. Where have you been?'

Alarms went off in my head. As far as she was concerned I'd just been at work and she hadn't reacted like this on other days I'd been working. I needed to stall for time.

I stepped inside and slowly closed the door behind me. I couldn't think straight as my brain was set in scream mode. I needed to clear my head to think.

'Well?' Mum demanded.

'Well what?' I said, hoping I could put her off. But it had the opposite effect.

'You know jolly well what. Where have you been? And before you feed me the line that you've been at work, I know you haven't.'

I gulped. She knew?

'It was so embarrassing. I went past the shop to check that you'd got there OK…'

Wait? What? 'You checked up on me?'

'Yes, I always do. I walk past the shop, peep in and then walk on. I like to know you're safe.'

'This is like living in a dictatorship!' The words were out before I knew it. I wanted to pull them back in on a string, unsay them.

'How could you?' Mum spat. 'I work my fingers to the bone – to the bone, looking after you – it's my *job* to make sure you're safe. And here you are, not giving one thought to your safety. Not considering how I might feel. I hadn't a clue where you were. All day I've been worrying where you might be, who you might be with, what you might be doing. You could have been kidnapped, snatched off the streets and I wouldn't have known. Murdered in a ditch.'

Mum was shouting now and her face was purple.

'So, I went into the deli and asked the lady behind the counter where you were.'

I shut my eyes. The world turned inside out. It wasn't supposed to happen like this. I'd only gone to Plymouth. I hadn't done anything illegal.

'When I tell her I'm your mum, she offers me her sincere condolences. You can imagine both our faces when I have to say I don't know what she's talking about. I have never been so embarrassed or so ashamed of you.'

I pulled open the front door again, and ran out.

'Come here this instant!' my mother screamed.

But there was no way I was going back. I didn't know what to say to her. I just wanted it all to stop. How did I manage to get my life into these knots? I tried so hard to make sure everyone was happy, that I was following the rules, and for what? It was all a total waste of time.

I could still hear Mum shouting as I reached the end of the street and turned down towards the town. I needed quiet so I could think. The buzz in my head wouldn't stop. It was like I had a radio playing which only I could hear. Telling me I was wrong, that I'd made the wrong decision, said the wrong thing, not pleased enough people. I wanted it to shut up. How did I make it stop?

I ran along the quay, to our bench. The rain was still hammering down, but the bench was under a tree, so it was protected from the worst of it. I slumped down, my legs feeling heavy. My back ached. I bent over, my head in my hands. I didn't know what to do. Mum was mad with me, Dad would know soon if he didn't already and he'd pull his 'I'm deeply disappointed in you' face and Wendy – happy, lovely, thoughtful Wendy, who'd given me the job, who'd altered my apron, who I'd lied to – she would hate me now. Who wouldn't?

The water was choppy in the estuary, white crests on the wave tops. Why couldn't I be better at life? No one else had these problems. Everyone else seemed to be able to manage, why couldn't I? Mum was going to ground me for sure after this. I wouldn't be allowed out. I would lose my job. My parents would hate me. And I wouldn't be able to see my friends for the rest of the holidays.

My friends. They'd understand, wouldn't they? I

couldn't go to Cam, not at the moment, she had enough to deal with. But Hetal and Sasha – they'd know what to do.

Me: *Hey H & S, you've got to help me out. This summer's a nightmare. I can't talk to Cam at the moment – she's got a crisis going on, but I'll let her tell you about it when she's ready. It's my mum – she's found out that I lied to go to Plymouth today. She thought I was at work. I told work I was at a funeral. But everyone's found out everything. I'm sat on our bench and I don't want to go home, and I don't want to go anywhere. I know this was supposed to be the summer of #NoRegrets, but I'm kind of regretting that now. I wish I'd never got the job, wish I'd just done what my mum wanted. That wouldn't have been so hard, would it? Would have saved everyone being so mad with me. Can't wait for you guys to get home. I'm missing you so badly xxx*

The pain in my chest was getting tighter and my breath was short. It felt like my body was being crushed. What was happening to me? I rubbed at my right arm. Shooting pains ran down to my fingers, which were tingling like I'd put them into hot water after being out on a cold day. My breath was hard to catch.

I was dying. I was having a heart attack and I was going to die here on this bench. The noises in my head were still chattering on, never shutting up, not stopping.

'Are you alright, dear?' asked an elderly woman from under her umbrella.

I shook my head. The pain was so bad I couldn't speak. All I could feel was the pain in my body, tightening across my chest, the pain when I tried to gasp a breath, the pain in my arms. I was going to die and everyone hated me. I'd messed it all up. And now I was going to mess it up even worse by dying on a bench I wasn't allowed to be on, by the sea I wasn't supposed to be anywhere near.

I could hear a siren in the distance. It was getting louder. Perhaps it was just another noise in my head. I saw an ambulance driving through the car park, blue lights flashing. Was that for me? I closed my eyes and wrapped my arms around my chest. I just had to hang on till they got to me.

CHAPTER 21
HETAL

I snuck back to my cabin between sessions. There'd been a question about amino acids and I wanted to double-check the facts. Pulling out my textbooks, I looked up the relevant chapters and, skim-reading through the details, I confirmed I'd been right. That was reassuring. I piled them carefully back into my locker. Before I went, I quickly checked my phone for messages. There was a strict no phones in sessions policy.

One from Nell thirty minutes ago was flashing. I clicked on it and read. She'd never sent a message like that before, she sounded really upset.

I tried calling her, but after ringing it went to voicemail. A tiny seed of worry sprouted in my mind. She wouldn't do anything silly, would she? Of course not, it was Nell. Always sensible. But she'd sounded so desperate. What could I do? I was stuck here. I rang her mum's mobile. I'd been given her number when she'd taken us out for the day once.

She answered. 'Yes?' She sounded flustered.

'Hello. It's Hetal.' I didn't know what to say so I just blurted it out. 'Is Nell alright?'

'Hetal? Oh. Look, I can't talk now, I've just heard that Nell's been taken to hospital. I've got to go.' The phone went dead.

Adrenalin surged through my veins. In hospital? What on earth had happened? There was no use in trying Nell's phone again. I felt so useless I could scream, trapped here, not knowing, not being able to help.

I knew in an instant what I wanted to do. I called my mum and told her I was coming home, that I would get a lift. Then I texted Cam and Sasha.

Me: *C&S – just spoken to Nell's mum. Nell's been*
       taken to hospital. I don't know why. I'm
       coming back from camp now. Love you xxx

I packed my bag and ran to the camp office. Josh was super-understanding and rang a taxi for me. My hands were shaking badly. I was desperate to see Nell. What could be wrong? Was it something to do with her arm? Or had she had an accident? It might be nothing, I tried to tell myself. I could be rushing for nothing, but no matter how rational and logical I tried to be, it didn't stop me shaking.

'The taxi's going to be twenty minutes,' said Josh. 'No point in waiting here. Why don't you nip down to the canteen and grab some tea and cake. I'll keep an eye on your stuff.'

I thanked him and hurried to the dining hall. It was the break between sessions and the hall was heaving with everyone trying to get drinks and some of the good cake.

Maddy came up to me. 'I wondered where you'd gone. Everything OK?' She looked at my face. 'It's not, is it?'

I shook my head. 'I've just heard that one of my best friends has been taken into hospital. I don't know why. A taxi is coming in a few minutes. I'm going home.'

'Oh Hetal, I'm so sorry.' She wrapped her arms around me. I held onto her, not sure if my legs were going to keep me upright on their own.

'Before you go, give me your number. It'd be great to keep in touch.'

I scribbled it down on a napkin, the numbers looking all squiggly because my hands wouldn't stop shaking.

'Thanks,' she said. 'Looks like someone else missed you last session.' She nodded towards Finn, who was looking over at us.

I realised that by leaving, I'd forfeit the trophy for overall winner. Finn would win it, no doubt. A tiny pang of sadness pulled at my heart. But he was worthy. I smiled over at him, and he smiled back.

'Why don't you tell him you're going?' said Maddy, nudging me towards him. 'You know you'll regret it if you don't.' Her words made me catch my breath.

Pulling together the last of my shredded nerves, I walked over to Finn. He was still smiling at me.

'I'm leaving,' I said. His smile vanished.

'What? Now?'

'Yes. My friend's in hospital.'

'Oh. Right.' He stood, shuffling his feet a bit. 'I'll miss you.'

'You will?'

'Of course. You're, well, you're awesome. I've never met anyone like you before.'

I stared at him. My brain had crashed.

'Hetal!' called Josh. 'Your taxi's here.'

'Got to go.' I hurried out of the hall. I could already feel regret seeping through me because I'd left that conversation unfinished. All the things I'd left unsaid. I stopped. I didn't want that regret.

I walked back into the hall, up to Finn, who had a surprised look on his face. My hands were shaking anyway, so it didn't matter if it was for a different reason now. I leaned up on my tiptoes and kissed him.

'Maddy's got my number,' I said.

Then before I could combust, I rushed from the dining room a second time. No regrets. I flew along the paths, back to the office and dived into the waiting cab. Josh had already put my bags into the car and he shut the door behind me.

'Hope your friend's OK,' he called as the car pulled away. Finn came running up behind him, and I could see them both waving as the car drove me down the road. Away from the bubble of camp and back into the real world. Back to my parents, back to my nani and back to my friends.

I fiddled with the tassels on my hoodie as I checked and checked my phone. Still no word from Nell. Or Cam and Sasha. Where was everyone? I hated not knowing. I sat in the back of the car, willing the driver to speed up, willing him to get me to the station in time to catch the earlier train.

'You heading home, are you?'

'Yes,' I said.

'Science camp not for you then?'

'Oh no. It's not that. It's just my friend...' My voice stuttered to a stop.

He must have sussed I didn't want to talk as he kept quiet after that, which gave my brain space to rampage. I was fighting the urge to list all the awful reasons Nell could be in hospital. It wasn't going to help. I had to stay calm. I leaned my head back against the headrest. Square breathing would help – the symmetry of it pulled me in.

I breathed in 2, 3, 4.

Held my breath 2, 3, 4.

Breathed out 2, 3, 4.

Held again 2, 3, 4.

I clung to the numbers and the rhythm until I felt my muscles relax and my heart rate slow. I had to be calm for Nell.

CHAPTER 22
CAM

Boris knew I was sad. He had always known when I was, ever since I first arrived at Jackie and John's. He was grey around his muzzle now and there were thin patches on his back, but he still knew when something was wrong. He laid his head on my lap, his eyes twitching up to look at me. I stroked his head. Jackie knew too. She'd brought me a hot chocolate with marshmallows – her remedy for most of life's problems.

She eased herself into the chair opposite the sofa.

'Cam? Are you going to tell me what's going on? And don't tell me it's nothing, because it's as plain as day that there's something wrong. Did you fall out with Nell?'

'No.' How could I tell her? She'd be so upset.

'Listen,' said Jackie, 'whatever it is, we can sort it. But I can't help if I don't know. There's nothing you can say that's going to change how I feel about you.'

I looked into her dark eyes and knew that what she said was true. She was one of the world's good people.

'I met my birth father today,' I said quietly. I let the words hang. It was no longer a secret. Jackie said nothing. Her face didn't change.

'I found him online. I knew his name was Phil Mirren. Mum had told me that, years ago. I don't know what made me start looking. Curiosity, I guess. Wanting to know where I come from? Perhaps to have someone in my life when I'm thirty. He works at a company in Plymouth, so me and Nell went and waited outside, to see if he'd come out at lunchtime.'

Jackie still said nothing. I closed my eyes, remembering what had happened. Remembering his face.

'He had my eyes.' My voice cracked a little. I heard a shuffle and Jackie sat down on the sofa next to me.

'That must have felt a bit ... funny,' she said. 'Did it?'

I nodded, looking at her now. 'Really weird. When I saw his picture online I knew I'd got the right person because he looked exactly like me.'

'Did you talk to him?'

I nodded again. 'I know it's not the way I should have done it. I wasn't even sure that I would speak to him. I didn't want to cause a big fuss and then decide I didn't want to do anything about it. I was only there to see him.'

'But when you saw him, you went and spoke to him?' said Jackie.

'Yes. I had so many questions. And I wanted to hear what his voice sounded like. Does that sound corny?'

'Not at all.'

'But when I said who I was, he went all funny. Said I wasn't to contact him again. Never again.'

I didn't feel like crying, but I could feel sadness sitting on me like a rock. Why would someone not want to know their own daughter? It didn't make sense.

Jackie put her arm around me. 'Oh, sweetheart.' She squeezed me tight. 'There'll be a reason why he said that, I'm sure.'

'But like what?' I felt like shouting. What could possibly be more important?

'You might have surprised him. He'd popped out for a sandwich and found a daughter. Not what you'd call a usual lunch break.'

I guess. Nell had said something similar.

'Or he might have felt embarrassed that he didn't know, or hadn't been involved. People can get pretty good at lying to themselves, but when the truth presents herself, they react in some very strange ways.'

She might have a point.

'What do you want to do now?' Jackie asked.

I looked at her. What did she mean, what did I want to do?

'He said I mustn't contact him again.'

'We could get your social worker involved. She'll be able to find out more. Register your interest to meet him should he change his mind. Act as a mediator.'

I nodded. That sounded good. I wouldn't have to do it. Someone would make my case for me.

'You should have told us,' said Jackie. 'It could have gone really badly. You could have been hurt. You didn't know anything about him. But that said, I can't help feeling so proud of you, Cam.'

She was smiling. She was proud of me?

'You've had a tough start in life and you are

turning into the most incredible young woman in front of our eyes. I can't believe how confident and strong you are. And if your birth father decides he doesn't want to know you, it is all his loss. Because those of us who are privileged to know you, know that you are a caring, fiercely loyal person.'

Her eyes were shining. I blinked a bit. Must be an eyelash.

'But never too big for a hug,' she said and hugged me tight. Boris got all excited and woofed between us. I laughed and scratched his ears. My heart still ached but the heaviness was gone.

When Papa John got in, we had tea together, the three of us, and he made us laugh about a customer who'd come in, a plumber who'd made even a blocked drain seem funny.

As I was clearing the table, I reached for my phone. I ought to text Nell to say thanks for getting me home OK.

I'd had a message from Hetal a couple of hours ago. As I read it, my blood ran cold. Nell was in hospital? But she'd only been with me this afternoon. Only a few hours ago. And she'd seemed all right. Hadn't she? Perhaps there had been something wrong and I'd missed it, so wrapped up with my own stuff. I was a totally crappy friend.

Hetal was on her way to the hospital.

'Jackie, John, I've got to go. Nell's in hospital.'

'What?' said Papa John.

Jackie looked shocked. 'Come on, I'll drive you.'

I followed her out of the door. It had started raining again. What could be wrong with Nell? Would today be a day I'd always regret for another reason? I shouted at myself to shut up. Who cared about my stupid regrets? It was Nell that mattered now. Nothing else.

CHAPTER 23
SASHA

The flight had been bumpy and the flight staff grumpy but I didn't care. I was going home. I couldn't wait to see Mum. I wondered if Dad had noticed I wasn't there yet. I'd half expected someone to come running up as I was boarding to say I wasn't allowed to go, or that my father was waiting outside to speak to me. But there was no running, no nothing. I suppose it wasn't that late and Dad wasn't in the habit of waking me in the mornings.

As the plane bumped along the runway at Exeter airport, I turned my phone on. A flurry of messages pinged up.

Dad: *Where are you? I am worried sick. Please ring.*
Please text. I love you. I'm sorry if I have upset
you. Please get in contact.

Dad: *I'm going out looking for you. If you get back to*
the apartment, please stay there. I love you x

Dad: *Natasha. Please ring me. I just want to know*
you're safe. You don't have to say where you are.

There were seventeen missed calls from him. He
had noticed then. Good. Perhaps leaving him to
stew a bit longer might be an idea.

There were also twenty-three missed calls from
Mum.

Mum: *Darling. Whatever has happened, we can sort*
it. I love you. Please ring me. Or text.

Mum: *Please. Sasha, I'm begging you. Ring me.*

Mum: *Is it something I've done? I'm so sorry if it is.*
Text me.

Mum: *If you've met someone on the internet,*
remember, they're not always who they say they
are.

I felt a bit sick reading Mum's. She tried so hard not
to come across as the worried mother, but I knew
she was. And to be honest, I'd given her a pretty

good reason to be worried – going AWOL in another country would do that.

In between the frantic texts from my parents was one from Nell. She sounded bad. Really bad. I was glad I was nearly home. I scrolled down to Hetal's text. I only had to read it once. I stood up, pulled my bag from the overhead locker and started pushing my way through the people. I had to get to the hospital.

Once I was finally out of the airport and in a taxi, I called Mum. She answered before the phone even rang once.

'Sasha? Is that you?'

'Hi Mum,' I said.

She burst into tears. I hadn't meant for her to get upset. Honestly, I hadn't. I guess I was so busy thinking about getting away from the Dad and Clarisse love party and the whole Pierre disaster that I hadn't given Mum a second thought.

'Sorry, Mum,' I said. 'I'm fine. No need to panic.'

She was laughing but still crying. She sounded a bit hysterical.

'No. No one's panicking. Where are you? Your dad and I have been so worried.'

'Sorry I've worried you, Mum,' I said again. I was not sorry I had worried Dad.

'Where are you?' I could hear her blowing her nose.

'In a taxi. I'm on my way back. I just landed in Exeter.'

Mum swore. Which is something I think I've only heard her do twice in my life. The other time was when Dad said he was leaving. I overheard them while they thought I was asleep, when I was really sitting on the stairs.

'I'm not coming straight home, though. Nell's in hospital. I don't know why, but I need to see her. I've got to be there.'

She was quiet.

'Mum? You still there?'

'Yes, love,' she said softly. 'You are coming home eventually?'

'Of course,' I nearly shouted. 'I've missed you like crazy and being with Dad was OK, but then his girlfriend turned up, and she's *soooo* young and they were, like, all over each other. Mum, it was totally gross. I thought I was going to throw up, like, most of the time. Then when I thought it was as bad as it could get, they announced their engagement. So, I did a bunk.'

'He did mention something like that.' I could tell she was holding her feelings in. She had very strict rules about not undermining Dad. I could imagine her face, concentrating on finding the best way of commenting.

'So, yes, I am coming home. I can't wait. But I have to see Nell first. Check she's OK. You do understand, don't you?'

'Completely,' she said.

'And will you let Dad know that I've come home. Suppose we'd best put him out of his misery.'

'I'll ring him straight away. He's been worried sick.'

That's odd. Not like Mum to be *that* concerned about Dad's feelings.

'See you soon then.'

'Yes, bye, love.'

'Bye, Mum.'

I texted the gang.

Me: *I'm on my way to the hospital too xxx*

I peered out of the window. It was chilly and raining. Such a difference from the heat of Geneva, but I loved it. The roads started to become more familiar. Soon we were on the outskirts of the town, driving through the streets that I knew inside out. The taxi pulled into the hospital drop-off zone, I paid and hopped out to get my bag. Just as I was hauling it onto the pavement, I heard a shout.

'Sasha, over here!'

It was Hetal. She was pulling a case too. She waved. I ran over and hugged her.

'You've come straight from science camp?' I asked.

'I left as soon as I saw her message and spoke to her mum. How come you're here? I thought you were still in Switzerland?'

'I was. Long story. Come on. Let's go and find Nell.'

We trundled in, dragging our cases behind us. Where would she be? Would we be allowed to just wander in and see her? I spotted a pink-haired girl at the information desk.

'Oi, Cam!' I called. The pink head turned.

'What?' screamed Cam. 'I thought you guys were both miles away. How the hell have you made it back so quickly? Oh, sod it. I'm just so glad to see you.' And she hugged us.

The woman behind the desk drummed impatiently with her nails.

'Sorry,' I said to the woman. 'Can you tell us if Nell Cooper is here, please?' If it was something major, they could have taken her to the big hospital, but surely she'd be here? The other one was miles and miles away.

The woman tapped on her keyboard and checked the screen. 'She's been moved to the ward. Straight down the corridor, last door on the left.'

We all ran off in the direction she'd pointed in, Hetal shouting, 'Thanks,' over her shoulder.

We got to the ward door.

'Is anyone else nervous?' asked Cam. 'Hospitals give me a funny feeling.'

I knew what she meant. Us being here to see Nell brought back memories of her accident. Please may she be OK, please may she be OK, I kept repeating in my head. She had to be OK. She was Nell. She always bounced back.

I pushed the door to the ward open and we walked in. At the nurses' station, I asked which bed was Nell's. A friendly nurse, who looked like she was juggling a dozen different tasks, pointed at a bed near the window. I realised that Nell's mum and dad were sitting on chairs beside the bed.

I gulped. Please may she be OK.

CHAPTER 24
NELL

I must have dozed off, exhausted from the pain. Even when I woke up again, I didn't open my eyes. I knew Mum and Dad were there and, if I opened my eyes, I'd have to face them. They'd wired me up to a monitor and the *blip blip blip* was quite a reassuring noise. I'd been moved to the ward, but the doctor had said it was precautionary. I'd heard him explaining it all to my parents. Stress, possibly post-traumatic stress disorder since the accident, all perfectly normal, very treatable, not as scary as it sounds.

The pain had stopped by that point and the relief of having now only an aching body, not a deadly painful one, had made me really sleepy.

'I'm sorry. She's asleep,' I heard my mum say. 'You'll have to come back later.'

I opened one eye a tiny crack to see who it was.

There, at the end of my bed, looking totally amazing, were Cam, Hetal and Sasha. What the hell?

'What on earth are you doing here?' I was so surprised I sat straight up in bed.

Mum jumped. 'Don't worry, love, you don't have to talk to them if you don't want to,' she said, her eyes on Cam's pink hair.

'Not want to talk to them?' I said. 'Oh, I've missed you so much.'

Hospital policy stated that you were not allowed to sit on patients' beds but my friends either didn't know or didn't care. It was a hug pile-on and it was the best hug I've ever had. I couldn't believe that a few hours ago I'd felt so alone and now I was drowning in friends.

'These are your friends?' Mum sounded shocked. She knew Hetal, of course, but Sasha and Cam were coming as a bit of a surprise.

'How about we go get a coffee?' said Dad to her. She didn't move. 'Come on,' he said again and gently but firmly steered her out of the ward.

'What are you guys doing here? I thought you were in Switzerland, Sasha?' How long had I been in here?

'I was on my way back already,' she smiled. 'But what about you? You gave us a bit of a scare.'

'You can say that again,' said Cam.

'Sorry. I'm not exactly sure what happened. Doctors think it was a panic attack. Honestly, though, it felt like I was having a heart attack. I thought I was going to die.'

Everyone was quiet for a minute.

Hetal spoke. 'It's true. I read an article about panic attacks. The pain you feel is very similar.'

'Woah, scary stuff,' said Cam.

'How are you feeling now?' asked Sasha.

'Better. Much better. It's all calmed down again now. They've put me on this thing, just to make sure.' I pointed at the monitor. They all looked at it. I watched their faces. They all looked so serious. I hated making everyone worry about me. I wanted them to forget that we were in a hospital and just act like we were sitting on our bench, messing about, chatting.

'How was Switzerland?' I asked Sasha. She was looking like she'd seen some sun. Her face shone and I spotted strap lines across her shoulders.

'Oh, Switzerland was awesome. Shame I had to be there with my dad, that's all.'

More silence. I wondered what had happened.

She'd mentioned in her texts about his girlfriend. But Sasha had her arms folded so I decided not to push it.

'I kissed a boy,' Hetal suddenly blurted out.

'You did what?' Cam cried. 'I want details. *You* kissed *him*? He didn't kiss you?'

Hetal was grinning crazier than I think I've ever seen her grin before.

'When? Was it a science geek? No offence,' said Sasha.

Hetal's grin didn't waver. 'It was this afternoon…'

Cam shrieked. A nurse tutted from across the ward.

'I'd decided I was leaving. I knew you were in hospital, Nell, so I'd packed up and just had time for a cup of tea.'

Sasha squealed. 'You kissed him over a cup of tea? Oh, I don't believe you, Hetal – you are living the dream, girl.'

Hetal laughed. 'He said he liked me. Then I had to leave. But then I realised I was already regretting not saying anything back. So I ran back, kissed him, told him to call me and left.'

Sasha was laughing hard. 'I bow before your greatness – you are totally awesome!'

Cam clapped her hands. 'Brilliant. Just brilliant.'

I looked around the ward. We were making a huge racket. The nurses kept looking over at us. I could feel a wave of noise building in my head and my stomach clenched.

'Guys, we've got to keep it down.'

They stopped instantly and looked at me.

'We're in a hospital,' I said. 'People are sick.'

They all smiled and nodded, and lowered their voices, but I felt worse. I bet they hated me now. I'm such a killjoy. Always safe and sensible. Obeying the rules. I still felt twitchy about them sitting on the bed. There was a massive sign saying they weren't allowed to.

Oh, how I wished I could ignore the rules. Follow the big ones, the important ones, but not care about the rest. But I couldn't tell the difference. Was the sitting on beds one a big one? Bet it was to do with infection or something. Argh, why did I care so much about every stupid damn thing?

'What do you think, Nell?' said Cam.

I blinked. I hadn't been listening.

'Sorry. What were you saying?'

I saw Sasha and Cam exchange a glance. It was only a tiny one, but I saw it. And when Cam spoke to me, it was slower than normal.

181

'Just wondering, if you're feeling up to it, whether we could go out somewhere next week, on the boat, or into Plymouth.'

There was no way Mum was going to let me out of the house without some sort of tracking device. She'd be double-checking everything I told her and, besides, she'd never let me near the sea, or go as far away as Plymouth.

'I might have to take a rain check,' I said. 'But you guys go ahead without me.'

I didn't want to stop them enjoying the holidays. It didn't have to be a nightmare for all of us.

CHAPTER 25
HETAL

Waking up in my own bedroom, instead of the camp cabin, was glorious. I scrooched down under my duvet and sighed. Home felt so good. Downstairs I could hear Nani singing along to the radio and the smell of a late breakfast was tickling my senses. It smelled like she was cooking the works. Well, it would be rude not to go down and eat it.

Pulling on my dressing gown, I headed to the kitchen.

'Morning, my gorgeous,' said Nani, wielding two frying pans. 'Sleep well?'

'Yes, thanks. That smells amazing.' She was making pancakes. The Indian sort. Nani calls them dosa and they are to die for.

'Thought you might like them.' Nani checked

both pans on the hob. I spotted a pile she'd made already in the oven. 'So?' she said. 'I want to hear all about it.'

I made us both some tea and we chatted and cooked and ate and chatted.

'How's your friend doing?' I asked Nani once I'd eaten one more dosa than I should have.

'Elsie? She's quite well at the moment, she says. She emailed only yesterday. She's off on a tour to see all her family, while she's still well enough. She's going all round the world.'

'Is she coming to the UK?'

'No, unfortunately not. The nearest she gets is Paris. Her son and daughter-in-law live there.'

I sighed, sad for Nani.

'What are you going to do today?' asked Nani. 'First day back – there must be lots of things you've got planned.'

To be honest, I hadn't really. I was still supposed to be at science camp. I thought about what everyone there would be doing now. Maddy would be stocking up at breakfast before rushing off to her first session, late and chatting non-stop. The thought made me smile. Finn would be there already, catching my eye as I walked in late with Maddy. Was I seriously missing being there?

I thanked Nani for breakfast and went upstairs.
Finding my phone, I checked the messages.

Nell: *I'm home! Doctors didn't think it was*
        anything serious so was sent home last night.
        Thanks for coming to see me – it was so good to
        see you all. Sorry if I seemed a bit spaced.

Cam: *No worries, glad you're home. Take it easy*
        OK?

Sasha: *You're home! Awesome – now we don't have to*
        break you out! Xx

I typed an answer.

Me: *Yay for being home, Nell. I'm also enjoying*
        being home – I have missed my bed x

Sasha: *Haha. You and your bed* ☺

My phone pinged. I expected it to be one of the
gang. But it wasn't. It was a number I didn't recognise.

        Hi. So I'm texting rather than calling, as
        actually ringing people while you're in a session
        is frowned on. And I'm hoping I'll get a trophy
        for paying attention. Hence texting under a
        book. Hope your friend is OK. Finn x

I grinned. He was thinking about me. And that little kiss on the end. That was hopeful.

Me: *You've got to stop texting in sessions. You don't want to miss out on that trophy by screwing up your last day x*

I waited. I could see he was replying.

Finn: *Ha. Funny. But not a chance. That trophy is in the bag. Missing you though. Science camp isn't the same without its star geek x*

If I ever needed to prove the theory 'a text can make you blush' I'd done it.

Me: *Missing you too xx*

I hesitated before putting the double kiss. It was an obvious escalation of emotion, but I thought Finn could handle it.

Finn: *xxx*

I bounced off my bed, got dressed and floated off into my day. Despite the rain clouds, there was nothing going to dampen my spirits.

That evening, after tea, my phone pinged.

Finn: *Want to know who won the Science Camp trophy? X*
Me: *Was it you? It was you, wasn't it? X*
Finn: *Well, yes, obvs ☺ x*
Me: *Congratulations! You totally deserve it x*
Finn: *I feel kinda bad. You deserve it too x*

I paused. I had really, *really* wanted to win it, so why didn't I feel gutted?

Me: *I'm amazed they didn't award it to me for my obvious awesomeness ☺ x*
Finn: *If it's any consolation the trophy's not that great x*
Me: *That makes me feel a whole heap better. Let's see it then x*

Finn sent through a picture of him kissing a massive gaudy gold cup. There was due to be a huge party as it was the last night and he looked ready to celebrate.

Me: *Wow! Dodged a bullet there! What a monstrosity x*

Finn: *Honestly, you have to see this thing up close to comprehend the full horror of the tat. Could I come and visit later in the holidays and share the awfulness? And you know, catch up x*

My heart skipped a beat. Did catch up mean catch up, or was it more? But I didn't care.

Me: *Sounds great! Xx*

Finn: *Cool xxx*

So that was decided then.

'Who you texting?' asked Dad.

'Just a friend from camp,' I said. I didn't need questions, especially when I didn't know the answers. I wasn't used to that. But as I sat there, listening to Mum, Dad and Nani, I decided it was OK. It was OK not to know the answer to everything all the time. I'd find out sooner or later.

CHAPTER 26
CAM

I sat beside Jackie as she rang social services. We'd left it a few days. Jackie said it was always best to have some thinking time before making any big decisions and, despite my impatience to get on with it, in the end I had to admit she was right. With a few nights' sleep, and a few days' thinking, I wasn't feeling so panicky.

'Hi, it's Jackie,' she said, when someone answered the phone. 'I've rung about Cam. No, there's nothing wrong. She's doing great. Couldn't be more proud of her.'

I rolled my eyes. Jackie could be a bit over the top in her pride. Jackie grinned at me.

'It's about her birth father.'

Jackie stopped and listened, umming and ahhing every few seconds. 'Oh, that's interesting.'

'What?' I whispered.

Jackie waved me away with her hand. 'Oh really? Yes, I see. Well, I'll talk to Cam. See what she thinks. I'll let you know. Great. Yes. Thanks. Bye.' She finally put the phone down.

'What did they say? You didn't tell them anything about my father.'

'I didn't need to,' she said. 'He's already been in contact with them. Seems he feels he was a bit hasty in his reaction to you last week. He sends his apologies. He is very keen to meet with you, if you feel able to give him a second chance.'

I had no words. He was sorry?

'And he has asked if you would like to go round to his house – with me, of course – to meet him properly.'

I opened my mouth. Then shut it again.

'And his wife. And their two children.' Jackie was watching me closely.

He was married. I don't know why that surprised me, but it did. And kids? That totally blew my mind. My father had other kids. Why had that never occurred to me before? There was no reason he wouldn't have other kids. He must have been super-young when he met my mum.

'So?' asked Jackie. 'What do you think?'

'Well,' I started, 'that's great. Isn't it?' I was worried now. It all seemed a bit too good to be true.

'It is very hopeful.' Jackie smiled. 'But, remember, we mustn't try to run before we can walk. It can take a long time to build up a relationship.'

Especially when you have luck like mine. Though, since moving in with Jackie and John, my luck had definitely improved.

'OK, let's do this. Let's go and meet them.' I felt a pang of panic. What if he repeated what he said the other day? 'You will come too, though?'

Jackie squeezed my hand. 'I'll be with you every moment.' I think she understood.

Jackie rang social services back and a meeting was arranged for the following day. Jackie seemed surprised it was so soon but wrote down the address while chatting to the social worker. I chewed on my fingernail. Surely the meeting being sorted so quickly could only mean good things. I wondered what it would be like. Would it be awkward? Probably. How could it not be? But would I regret going? I couldn't imagine it. This was what was going to happen, and I was happy with it. Didn't mean I wasn't nervous as hell, though.

I was pacing up and down the hall fifteen minutes before we had to leave the next morning. Papa John was going to work late so he could see us off.

'You alright, kid?' he said from his chair in the lounge as I passed the door for about the hundredth time.

'Yep. Just want to get on with it now. I can't stand all this waiting about.'

Papa John came into the hall. 'Patience,' he said. 'There's no point in turning up early.'

'Argh!' I cried. 'Why does time go so slowly when you don't want it to?'

'Cam,' he said. His face was twitching, as if he was trying to say something but finding the right words was causing him physical pain. 'Would you stop pacing like a wildcat? You're making me jumpy.'

I stopped. I was very nearly as tall as him. I could remember when I first arrived he'd seemed so much taller.

'That's better,' he said, and gave me a massive bear hug. 'I may not be your birth father, but I'll always be your papa, OK? Always.'

Surprised, I hugged him back, squeezing him tight.

When he finally let me go, he cleared his throat,

as if his words had been as much of a surprise to him as to me. 'Where's Jackie got to? She should be ready by now.'

'Here she is,' I said as she came down the stairs. She had her best dress on. I looked down at my scruffy jeans. Was I too underdressed? What if they didn't like me?

Jackie must have had her mind-reading skills turned up to max. 'You look great,' she said. 'Exactly how any sixteen-year-old should look in the holidays.'

I let my breath out with a whoosh.

'All set?' asked John.

'Yes.' Jackie nodded. 'Got the address, sat nav, emergency snacks.'

I don't think I could have eaten even if you'd paid me.

'Hope you get on OK.' John looked at me. I nodded. 'Just be yourself.'

Within half an hour we were standing on Phil Mirren's doorstep. In the estate of identical houses, it stood out with its sea-blue front door. Jackie rang the bell. I twisted my fingers together, waiting.

The door opened, and there he was. My father. Only instead of frowning this time, he had a nervous smile. The glimmer of hope burned a bit brighter inside me.

'Camille, Jackie, lovely to see you. Do come in.'

I stepped inside. It was a modern house with clean lines and lots of white paint. I took my shoes off. I felt like I was already making the place untidy.

'Come on through. Sue and the girls are dying to meet you.' He was looking at me properly this time. I tried to smile but it felt wobbly.

I followed him, Jackie behind me, into a big, sunny kitchen. The back door was open and I could hear kids playing outside. A woman came over and hugged me. Which should have felt weird.

'Camille, I'm so pleased to meet you. I'm Sue, Phil's wife. Can I get you a drink of something?'

'A cup of tea would be great, thanks. And call me Cam. Everyone does.'

Sue smiled at me. 'Cam it is.'

I perched on a small sofa while Jackie and Phil exchanged pleasantries about the traffic on the way here. The voices outside suddenly got louder and a small girl burst in from the garden.

'Mummy, Mummy, she's taken it again. And she won't give it back. Go and tell her off, Mum…'

She caught sight of me and stopped mid-sentence. The funny thing with kids is that they don't care about staring. And she stared right at me, her eyes like saucers.

'Hi, I'm Cam,' I said. I didn't know how much they'd been told about me.

'Oh yes, I know. You're our new big sister. And you have pink hair. I love pink. It used to be my favourite colour but now it's green. What's yours?'

She spoke quite clearly and without any worry or complication. It was so simple to her. I was her new big sister.

'Um, I think it's yellow,' I said.

'You only think? Don't you know?'

'Well, I haven't thought about it recently.'

The girl shook her head, obviously disappointed in my failure to colour-rank.

'Well, my favourite is green, then pink, then orange, then lilac. Not purple, lilac.'

'Sounds like you've got it all sorted,' I said.

'I have,' she said, nodding seriously.

Later, after I'd been shown Maisy and Erin's toys, their bedrooms and their garden, I sat down again with Jackie on the little sofa.

'You doing OK?' she said softly.

I smiled. I was. Maybe even more then OK. There were the odd moments of awkward but nothing overwhelmingly cringe. Maisy and Erin didn't let anything stand still long enough for there to be quietness.

'Cam,' said Phil, 'I'd like to make sure I say this. I know this is just an initial meeting, and you'll have to go away and think about how it's gone. But I want to apologise for what I said to you last time. You caught me off guard. I had no idea I had a daughter. I didn't know that your mum was pregnant. But that is no excuse. I was rude and abrupt and I am truly sorry for that.'

I nodded. 'That's OK. I guess it must have been quite a shock.'

Phil grinned. 'The best kind of shock. It's not every day you gain a daughter.' His enthusiasm was infectious, making me smile.

'You're kidding, right? I've gained a whole family. I'm totally mind-blown.'

He laughed.

'So, what happens now?' I said. It was the question I was most nervous about asking.

'Well, I guess we take it one step at a time.'

Sue was listening. I wondered how she felt about all this. She must have caught me looking. 'You are welcome any time,' she said, smiling. And, somehow, I knew she meant it.

At the end of the morning, Jackie and I left. As

we walked away from their front door, I waved to Maisy and Erin through the window. I was carrying the drawing Erin had done of me. Massive body, with loads of pink hair. They were cool kids. I felt I'd entered the lottery and won a bonus family.

CHAPTER 27
SASHA

Devon was cooler, rainier and way more laid back than Switzerland had been and I was loving it. I'd thrown myself into seeing my friends, spending time with my mum and checking if the local talent had improved while I was away. (It hadn't.)

Dad kept texting me, but other than a text telling him not to worry about it, I hadn't really replied. What was the point? I wasn't going to be seeing him again for ages, so it hardly seemed worth the bother of patching up the relationship. Let time do it. Why did I have to?

I poured Mum a cuppa as she walked in from work. 'Tea's made,' I called when I heard the door close behind her.

She came into the kitchen and put her bags

down. 'Thanks, love. Just what I needed.' She sat down and took a sip. 'Ah, that's good.'

I sat opposite her with my glass of orange juice.

'I've heard from your dad that you're not replying to his messages.'

'No, I haven't.'

'Can I ask why not?'

'I don't see the point. I'm not going to be seeing him for ages anyway.'

Mum put her mug down.

'This is your *dad* we're talking about. One of your two parents. Fathers don't grow on trees.'

Mum was never rude about Dad but it wasn't like her to stick up for him either. What had got into her?

'He was worried sick after he found you'd gone.'

'So?' I said. He'd deserved it. Hadn't he?

Mum reached out her hand and took mine.

'As you grow up, sometimes relationships need working at. A bit of effort, even when you think it isn't your turn or your place to put in the effort. That's what it's about. A bit of give and take.'

'What are you saying? That I shouldn't have left, that I should have stayed and put up with it?'

'No,' said Mum, 'that's not what I'm saying. Of course you could have come home, anytime you liked. But you should have let your dad know. He wouldn't have stopped you, but it would have prevented a huge amount of worry. For everyone.'

Huh.

'I think, perhaps,' said Mum, and I could sense where she was going as clearly as if she'd already said it, 'you should apologise and try to make it up with your dad.'

I rolled my eyes.

'You don't want to leave it so long that it becomes a Thing, and then it's been three years since you've seen him and you have no relationship left at all.'

I picked at my nail.

'Your dad's sorry, and perhaps he's suffered enough.'

After tea I went upstairs to my room. Mum's words were bouncing around my head like balls in a pinball machine. I didn't want to say sorry. But I didn't want to never see Dad again over it. I sat on my bed, holding my phone. I could call. Just to say hi.

It only rang twice.

'Hello? Natasha?' came Dad's voice.

'Hi Dad,' I said.

'Ah, it is so good to hear you. I have been so worried.' He sounded properly pleased. 'I thought we were having such a good time and then, *poof,* you were gone and it felt like my heart had been ripped from my chest.'

He'd felt like that?

'Sorry, Dad. I didn't mean to worry you. I just thought you and Clarisse would have a better time without me.'

'Never!' he said. 'And I am sorry if I made you think that.'

'And I'm sorry that I didn't tell you I was leaving.'

'Thank you, *ma petite*, I understand,' said Dad. 'And Clarisse? She maybe was a bit of a surprise too, *n'est-ce pas?*'

'You can say that again.'

'I am sorry, Sasha, you must believe me.' His voice was serious. 'I shouldn't have expected you to spend all that time with her. I assumed that because I love you both, that you would get along. It was insensitive of me.'

'I'm sorry too. I guess I could have been nicer to her. I was quite rude.' I paused, summoning the courage to say what I knew needed saying. 'Can you tell her I'm sorry?'

'Of course.' I could hear him smiling. 'How about we start again? A clean slate, no?'

'Sounds great, Dad.'

'Listen, I'm in the UK this week. How about I pop down to Devon to see you?'

I thought about it and what Mum had said.

'That would be nice.'

He turned up two days later, in an impossibly chic, cream linen suit. Mum was at work and I wasn't entirely sure what to do with him. But I needn't have worried.

'Natasha, seeing as I'm in town just for the day, would you do me the honour of being my tour guide?'

'Don't be daft, you lived here for years, you know it.'

'I might know the town, but I don't know *your* town. I want to see the bits that are important to you.'

His eyes had a twinkle of hope hiding behind a nervous smile.

'OK, you're on. But you better keep up. There's loads to see.'

I walked down the road beside him. He didn't try and link arms, but he kept asking me questions. Where do you catch the school bus from? (Three roads from our house.) What time do you go out in the mornings? (Bus comes at 7.50 so about ten minutes before that.) Were the neighbours still the same? (No, and the new ones are much nicer.)

I took him into town. Showed him the Harbour Bookshop where they knew what I liked to read and always kept books aside if they thought I might be interested in them. We walked up the hill and popped into Papa John's hardware shop, where I introduced him to Cam. All credit to Dad, he didn't flinch at the pink, he just shook her hand and murmured, '*Enchanté.*'

We stopped for a milkshake in Alley Cats, then looped back down, through the town and along the quayside to the second-to-last bench.

'This is where I meet up with my friends,' I said, sitting down. Dad sat beside me.

'It is a lovely spot.' He gazed out across the boats bobbing along the quay.

'It really is,' I said, breathing in deeply. I loved it here.

'What else is there to see?'

'Think that's pretty much it.'

'Well, thank you very much for showing me around. Now when I am miles away, I can picture where you are and perhaps imagine what you might be doing.'

'You think about me?' Somehow, I hadn't really thought about it.

'More than you know,' said Dad. 'I miss seeing you.'

'I miss seeing you too.'

We sat in silence for minute or so. A boat came chugging up the estuary and manoeuvred onto a waiting trailer before being hauled, dripping, from the water.

'I know you are not little anymore,' Dad said, 'and that you have more sophisticated tastes now.'

I looked at him, wondering where he was going with this.

'But I was wondering if you fancied an ice cream.'

I laughed.

'It has been years,' he said, 'since I've had a good British ice cream.'

'Yeah, I would love that.'

We wandered back along the promenade, stopping to buy two ice creams: bubble-gum flavour for me and rum-and-raisin for Dad. We walked along, eating our ice creams, round to the park.

'How about a game?' I said. It was another of the things we used to do before he left. The nine-hole putting green was unchanged. 'But I must warn you. I am significantly better than I used to be.'

'Challenge accepted,' said Dad.

When I saw him off that evening, he gave me a big hug.

'I will miss you, *ma belle*.'

'Miss you too, Dad.'

'How about you come and stay for a weekend sometime before Christmas? Marseille isn't all that far away, you know.'

'That'd be good,' I said. And I meant it. It would be a good opportunity to get to know Clarisse properly this time.

As the taxi drove away, Mum and I waved.

'I'm proud of you,' she said, looking after the disappearing car. 'It's not always an easy step to take but I'm glad you're mending the bridge.'

'Me too, Mum. Me too.'

Lying in bed that night, I realised it had been a good day. I'd enjoyed myself. It'd made my heart feel whole again, somehow, when I hadn't realised it was broken.

CHAPTER 28
NELL

The days after coming out of hospital were a blur of knotted emotions. I was maxing out on all the feelings and I'd have given anything to turn them down, like dimming the lights, or turning the music down. It was knackering. I should have listened to Mum. I should have followed the rules. What should I expect? I've got a prosthetic hand for crying out loud. Of course she was wanting what was best for me.

But does that mean I shouldn't have gone with Cam? Shouldn't have helped her when she went to find her father? And should I have told Wendy the truth? But it wasn't my truth to tell. Who should I please? Mum? Cam? Wendy? Me? All the things I should be thinking, ought to be doing, could have said were buzzing round my head like flies and I wanted to swat them all dead.

The therapist recommended by my GP had a clinic near Plymouth. She wanted to meet all of us on the first visit. Mum had asked if it was really necessary but, when the doctor insisted that it wouldn't harm, Dad booked the day off work and Mum had her hair done.

I already knew what she'd say, though. That I needed to stop lying, start doing what Mum says, stop expecting to do so much given my 'situation' (something she'd say in that whisper-voice people reserve for talking about disability, cancer and death). And, above all, cut out the worrying: it's bad for you.

I knew the theory. It's just in practice it was so damn hard.

In the car on the way, I looked at the back of my parents' heads. Dad had curls of grey twirling through his dark hair, and Mum sat, more hunched over than normal. When did we all get so squashed?

'Do you think we ought to talk about it before we get there?'

'Talk about what?' said Mum.

Dad concentrated on the road.

'Everything, anything,' I said. 'My panic attack, I guess.'

'Well, that's what the therapist is for. She'll sort it all out.'

'Look, I know if I'd done everything you'd told me, not seen my friends, not got a job, not gone to Plymouth, not sat beside the sea and just stayed at home, none of this would have happened. Maybe that's the answer. I'll just stay in, where it's safe.'

Mum said nothing. Dad still looked at the road. We carried on in silence. I hadn't really expected an answer – it was obvious that's what I should have done.

The waiting room had a vase of flowers on the windowsill and the scent of the sweet peas wafted on the breeze from the open window. A lady opened a side door. She had neat grey curls round her face and sharp eyes. She'd totally take my mum's point of view.

'The Cooper family, I presume?' She stepped forward, extending her hand. To my surprise, she shook my hand first. 'Very pleased you meet you, Nell.' she said. Her sharpness softened as she smiled. 'Come on through.'

We all followed her into her consulting room, which looked like someone's sitting room: easy chairs, coffee table, soft rug. It felt unexpectedly inviting. I chose a chair opposite the door. Mum, Dad and the lady sat down round me.

'Thank you for all agreeing to come along,' she said. 'We're all here to help you, Nell, and to help you as a family, to have strengthened relationships, and help improve your mental health.'

Dad nodded earnestly. This was *way* out of all our comfort zones.

'I see that the catalyst for coming to me was a panic attack, Nell. Can you tell me about that?'

I gulped. 'Well, I was on the quay.'

I looked sideways at Mum. Was she going to interrupt, say I wasn't supposed to be there? But she stayed quiet.

'I was sat on a bench. It was raining. There seemed to be like a roar, a lot of background noise. Like static. All the time in my head. Then my chest started really hurting, and I couldn't breathe. Someone must have called an ambulance.'

'And how did that feel?'

How did that feel? How did she think it felt?

'It felt scary. I thought I was going to die.' I could feel tears pricking in my eyes.

'Have you ever felt like that before?'

I nodded. A year ago. When I had my accident. I'd never really spoken about it. Every time I tried,

Mum would ask why I kept bringing it up. She said that it was over and I should just try and make the best of what I had.

'I should have followed the rules. I know now. The panic attack proved it. It wouldn't have happened if I'd not gone out.'

'But can you tell me about the other time you felt like that?' she asked again.

Mum couldn't keep quiet any longer. I knew she wouldn't be able to. 'We think it's best forgotten about. There's no use in bringing it up all over again, all that pain. Nell needs to move on, not look back.'

The lady noted something down, then placed her pen on the table.

'The reason we look back in these sessions is because sometimes what has happened in our past is affecting our present and has the potential to influence our future. Sometimes, if it's a traumatic or painful event, our brain doesn't know how to deal with it. This can lead to panic attacks, anxiety and depression. We need to look back in order to move forward.'

'But Nell's panic attack wasn't anything to do with her accident. It was because I'd caught her lying about where she'd been and who she'd been with. She even lied to her boss.'

I looked down into my lap. This is what I'd been dreading. But she was right. I'd lied to her and I'd lied to Wendy.

'I'm sorry, Mum. I'm sorry, alright?' My voice cracked. 'I'm sorry I didn't stay at home. If I hadn't gone out, I wouldn't have had a panic attack. And if I hadn't gone out a year ago, I wouldn't have had my accident. I get it now. I can't do what other people can.'

The room was silent for a moment.

'Mrs Cooper, would you mind if I asked you a question?' said the lady. Mum nodded, slowly. 'Do you feel under pressure a lot of the time? That you can "save" Nell by giving her strict rules to follow? That if only you knew where she was every minute of the day, you could keep her from ever getting harmed again?'

'No! I mean, no, of course not.' Mum was shaking her head.

I frowned. What did the therapist mean?

Dad cleared his throat. Both Mum and me turned to look at him. 'Look, love, I know it's hard. But don't you think you ought to say what you've been worried about?' He turned to check with the therapist, who nodded. 'There's no judgement here, but we've both been struggling since Nell's accident. To know the right thing to do. How to protect her.'

Mum covered her face with her hands. 'No one tells you being a parent is so hard.' She lowered her hands. 'I just want to do my best and I want to keep Nell safe *so badly* it's like a physical pain. I can't bear the thought of anything happening to her again.'

'You are by no means alone,' said the therapist. 'I've seen this countless times. Your family suffered a huge trauma. You are all reacting to it in different ways. All of these are perfectly normal reactions to have. But, if it's left to go on too long without acknowledging it, it has the potential to hold back not only your lives, but Nell's life as well.'

I couldn't take my eyes off her.

'So, are we stuck like this forever?' asked Mum. 'Because I feel like I'm going mad some days.'

This was news to me. Mum always seemed so sure of everything.

'You feel like that too?' I whispered.

Mum turned to me. 'Nearly all the time. That day of your accident.' She paused. 'I could never forgive myself that I'd allowed it to happen. You were a child. I'm your mother. It's my job to keep you safe. And I failed. I promised myself that I would never let that happen again. No matter what it took.'

'But Mum, you're suffocating me,' I said.

Mum nodded. 'I know. But I thought that was a price worth paying. Better to be alive and mad with your mother than dead.'

I put out my hand and held hers. She squeezed mine tight. 'It wasn't your fault, Mum.'

'I just love you so very much. I never wanted anything bad to happen to you.' A tear dripped down her cheek. She clasped my hand in both hers. 'I love you, Nell.'

'I love you too, Mum. I'm sorry I didn't understand.'

'How could you? I don't really understand myself.'

The lady was scribbling notes again.

'So then,' said Mum, sniffing, 'what can we do?'

The lady smiled. 'You're already making a great start. Talking about it, being willing to empathise, are essential if you are to work through the trauma. I think a few sessions together, encouraging you to talk openly will help. Then I can see you individually to deal with your personal situations and you should be well on the way.'

'Thank you,' said Dad.

'I have to warn you, this does not stop Nell being the age she is. She's sixteen, nearly an adult, and part of growing up is becoming independent and making decisions for herself. You can guide her as parents, but ultimately, it is her life, and she gets to have a say, if not the say.'

Mum looked at me and nodded. 'OK then. I'm up for this if you are?'

'Me too, Mum.'

'Right then,' said the therapist, 'let's get to work.'

After the session was over, we walked out into the sunshine towards the car.

'I thought that went very well,' said Mum, her face still blotchy.

I nodded. My head felt like it was going to explode. We got into the car and Dad pulled out onto the road.

'How are we going to make sure we keep talking, you know, about ... stuff?' I held my breath, hoping that Mum wouldn't dismiss me with an 'of course we will, don't be so silly'.

Mum turned round in her seat to look at me. 'Because I'm going to try every day. And if I try to listen, will you try to tell me? I can't promise I'll always get it right, but I can promise that I will try.'

I nodded. 'You're on.' That was a start. Perhaps there was a way we could work this out. Did it matter that I couldn't see how?

'But let's take it steady, a day at a time. We want to make sure you're strong enough before you do anything to really test you.'

'Sounds fair,' I said. And it did. A few quiet days, figuring things out would definitely help. We had another session booked, and life had a speck of hope in it again.

I thought about Wendy. I'd lied to her. A crushing guilt-wave crashed over me. Gorgeous, gave-me-a-chance Wendy. I could never fix that, but I had to apologise. There was no way I could live with myself if I didn't.

When we reached home I got out of the car. 'Mum, Dad, I've got to go somewhere.'

Mum took a deep breath. 'OK. Can I ask where?'

She was asking because she loved me. It made sense now.

'I need to talk to Wendy.'

Mum nodded. 'See you in a bit then, love,' she said. 'And Nell?'

'Yes?'

'We're both so proud of you, aren't we, Ted?'

Dad nodded.

'You guys are the best,' I said, quickly kissing them both before running off along the road. I needed to talk to Wendy before I lost my nerve.

I was out of breath by the time I got to the top of the high street. The lunchtime rush had gone, and I could see Wendy wiping down sides, well into her afternoon routine.

I pushed the door open and it jangled. She looked up.

'Hello.' My mouth was dry and I was shaking like I was in the queue for a roller coaster.

'Hello yourself.' She was eyeing me cautiously, as if not sure what to expect.

'I, um, I wanted to say I was sorry. I shouldn't have lied to you. Especially when you'd been so kind to me, and altered my apron, and everything. I'm sorry. And I know you won't want me to come back to work. But I didn't want not to say … well … sorry.' My voice trailed off.

'Your friend – Cam is it? – came in and explained why you needed the day off.'

'She did?'

Wendy nodded.

'I couldn't say. It wasn't my secret to tell.'

'I can see that,' said Wendy, 'and while I don't like you lying to me, I do understand why you did.'

'You do?'

Wendy nodded again.

216

'So, if you'd like to carry on working here, you can. But there's one condition.'

My heart jumped. I might get to keep my job? 'What?'

Wendy grinned. 'Sing with me!'

What?

'There's no way I'm singing.'

A boy came out of the back room. My cheeks flushed. It was the boy I'd tried to buy bread from when I didn't have any money. Was it possible to die from actual cringe? Crap – had he heard what I'd said? Did he know? My feet were twitching for the exit.

'You'd better sing with her. She won't stop hounding you until you do.'

Wendy swatted him with her tea towel. 'Tom, you might be my nephew, but you'll soon to be without a job, if you're not careful.' She fake-frowned at him, a smile hiding just beneath the surface.

He stuck his tongue out at her and carried on wiping the sides where Wendy had left off.

'Come to think of it,' said Wendy, 'this is the perfect opportunity for a staff team-building exercise. We'll all sing – that includes you, Tom.'

Tom grimaced, but he must be used to his aunt as he put his cloth down.

'Oh, come on,' she said to me, stepping out from behind the counter. 'It'll be fun.' She wacked up the music. 'Surely you know this one.'

I did. It was Gloria Gaynor. I gulped. What had I got to lose? Other than, you know, all self-respect.

'I know what we need,' said Wendy, grabbing a long baguette and snapping it in three. 'Microphones.'

Wendy handed me one piece and threw another to Tom who caught it. It was now or never: my #NoRegrets moment. I grinned at Wendy and, not daring to look at Tom, lifted the crusty loaf to my mouth. No matter what happened, I thought as I started to sing, I would survive.

Wendy put her arm round my shoulders, her voice much louder than mine, and Tom grinned as he joined in too.

CHAPTER 29
HETAL

I could hear Nani on the phone as I came downstairs. I wasn't meaning to listen, but sometimes the words just fall into your ears.

'Paris must be beautiful this time of year. And you're staying there for a few days? Oh yes, I see. Yes. Yes.'

I walked past her and into the kitchen. She was talking to Elsie. Must be. I didn't think she knew anyone else in Paris. Sasha had been talking about spending weekends in Marseille with her dad. She was saying how it really wasn't that far. But imagine going all that way for a weekend. Then I stopped, my milk mid-pour. Paris was closer than Marseille. And I was sure you could get there by train, through the Channel Tunnel.

I abandoned making my cup of tea and picked up my phone. Nani could go to Paris to see Elsie. She could get a train, so no flying. It was straight through from London so she wouldn't have to change in France. It was perfect. Within a few minutes I'd figured out how she'd get to London. I could go with her that far, just to make sure she was OK, then Elsie or her son could meet her at the other end. I was bouncing with excitement, desperate for Nani to get off the phone so I could suggest it to her.

Nani hung up and walked into the kitchen. 'Pop the kettle on, there's a love. All that chatting has dried me out.'

I flicked the switch and put a mug next to mine.

'Nani?' I said. 'I've had an idea.'

'Really? Let's hear it then.'

I stopped myself. Despite Nani having encouraged us to grab life, she may not like the idea of going to Paris. I could imagine her listing excuses. And, if I told her and she said no, that would be that. Nani could be very stubborn sometimes.

'Um, actually, it's nothing.'

Nani looked at me for a moment.

'Really. I thought it was an idea, but it's not.

Forget it.' I handed Nani her cup of tea and smiled at her. This needed to be very carefully planned.

That afternoon, as soon as the tide was high enough, Sasha, Cam and I went out on Papa John's boat. There wasn't much breeze, so we had to motor most of the way, but the three of us took it in turns on the tiller. The sky was cloudless and the sun shone down like it was supposed to.

Once clear of the estuary and onto open water, Cam anchored up and we leaned back, soaking up the sun and enjoying the gentle rock of the boat.

'Did I tell you what Maisy did yesterday?' said Cam.

'No,' I said, without opening my eyes.

'She gave me a card and she'd drawn a massive picture on the front. It had her mum and dad on it and her and Erin. And she'd drawn me, right in the middle.'

'That's cool.' It was odd, but in a good way, hearing Cam talk about her sister.

'How did you know it was you?' asked Sasha.

'Pink hair, obviously.' She sounded like she was smiling.

'So, things are going well then, with Phil?' said Sasha.

'Really well. I can't believe it. I keep wanting to pinch myself, just to check it's real. And I know, before you start, it might not always be perfect. Jackie keeps saying that. But, you know what? I'm going to flipping enjoy it while it is good.'

'Your no-regrets summer worked out then,' said Sasha. She was leaning back on her elbow, her hand tucked into her hair. 'What about you, Hetal? Have you got any regrets about our no-regrets summer?'

We all laughed.

I thought about it. 'Nope. I mean, I missed you all when I was at camp but, honestly, it was awesome. I'd never have known without trying. I had planned to go to Exeter or Plymouth for uni, so I could stay at home, but now … now maybe I'll try for Oxford or Cambridge.'

'You'd totally get in,' said Cam. 'They really love geeks there.'

I threw a towel at her.

'And you did meet Finn,' Sasha grinned. 'That's got to swing it.'

I laughed. 'Ah yes, I've got no regrets about Finn. What about you, Sasha? Was Switzerland a good thing?'

Sasha paused a moment. 'Well, I thought it was a massive mistake. I mean, I was trapped with my dad, who ignored me. Then there was his ridiculously young girlfriend – it was hardly in my top ten summers. But, I guess I do now have a better relationship with my dad and I am going to see him more regularly because of it, so perhaps it was worth it. And I totally fell in love with Switzerland. And travelling on my own was a killer buzz. Perhaps after my A-levels I'll barista my way round Europe for a year or two. So, no, despite it not all being amazing, there's no regrets from me.'

No one spoke for a moment, the only sounds were the lapping of waves on the hull and the distant squawk of a young seagull.

Cam was the one who said what we were all thinking. 'I'm not sure the no-regrets thing's worked out for Nell.'

Nell. Lovely, strong Nell.

'What did she say when you asked her to come along today?' I asked.

Cam frowned. 'She said she was having a few quiet days at home.'

'Sounds reasonable,' said Sasha.

'Sounds boring more like,' Cam replied. 'I'd go mad stuck in all day.'

'Perhaps she's just taking things steady.' I wasn't as sure as Cam. I liked being at home.

'Since when was meeting up with us hard work?' said Cam.

'Anxiety can make everything seem like hard work,' I explained.

Sasha had been listening to us.

'OK, so how can we help her?' she said. 'If there's one regret I don't want, it's that we didn't do everything we could to help her. And this whole afternoon has been lovely, but we're missing one of us. It feels wrong without her.'

She was right.

'We need to do something. The best thing to do is to keep texting, even if she doesn't always reply. Just so she knows we're here for her.' I would start as soon as I had a signal again.

Cam was nodding. 'OK, we'll keep in touch, be supportive. Think we can all manage that,' she said. 'Right, let's do what we came for – let's swim.' And she jumped into the water, making the boat rock violently. When she surfaced, she splashed water at us till we joined her.

CHAPTER 30
CAM

We were crammed into Hetal's room again, duvets and sleeping bags piled everywhere as they always are at sleepovers.

'What do you think? You can see my roots.' I pulled my hair apart so they could see the light brown showing through the pink. 'Do I have it re-done or let it grow out?'

'What do *you* want to do?' asked Sasha. 'That's the question.'

She was right. Did I want to start college with pink hair and be instantly labelled, or blend in with my oh-so-standard brown hair?

'I want pink hair,' I said. 'I feel like I've found my true self since I've had it done. And, besides, Maisy and Erin think it's cool and who am I to destroy their hero worship?'

Everyone laughed.

'I owe you one, by the way.' Nell's dark eyes were fixed on me. 'You talked to Wendy for me.'

'Don't worry about it. What did she say?'

'She was cool. Got to keep my job on one condition.'

'Which was?' said Sasha.

'I had to sing Gloria Gaynor with her.'

'What?' said Hetal.

Nell laughed. 'We used baguettes as mics. And that boy was there too. His name's Tom. Anyway, when we were done, she said, "Welcome back," and gave me the biggest hug, as if that was all completely normal.'

'She sounds like the nice sort of bonkers,' said Sasha.

Nell laughed again. 'She is.'

I've missed hearing Nell laugh. Sasha's right. We've got to find a way to keep Nell laughing. I'd not really realised what she'd been going through. She'd always seemed so happy to conform. I think of all of us, Nell had made the biggest changes, made the hardest choices, and had the toughest time this summer.

'You know, Nell,' I said, 'I think you're amazing. You are so much stronger than you think.'

Nell smiled a wobbly smile. 'Thanks. I think I'm getting better. Or at least I know what's going on in my mind, and that really helps. But it's hard.'

I thought back to her accident. How she'd appeared to bounce back so easily afterwards. Perhaps minds take longer to heal than arms.

'Well, I'm here for you. Whatever you need, whenever, OK?' I wished I could just magically make her feel better, but there was no quick fix. I vowed to be the friend who was going to be there for the long term.

'There's one person I think we need to stop from having a regret,' said Hetal.

'Really?' Sasha sat up. 'Who?'

'Nani.'

'What do you mean?' I asked.

'You know her friend, Elsie?'

We all nodded.

'Well, she's in Paris next week. She's doing a tour round all her family. Like a farewell trip, I guess. And she's at her son's in Paris.'

'Your nani could go and see her,' said Sasha.

'I know. But I reckon she won't want to.'

'Why not?' I asked.

Hetal shrugged. 'She wouldn't want to travel all that way on her own. I mean, I could go with her to the station in London and Elsie could meet her in Paris, but even the train might be too much.'

'That's a shame. She was so sorry she was never going to see her again,' Nell sighed.

'But this is the summer of no regrets. She was the one who inspired us,' I said. 'There's got to be a way to persuade her.'

We thought hard.

Then Hetal snapped her fingers. 'What if we all went with her? We could carry her luggage, make sure she got the right train, stuff like that.'

I looked at Hetal. She was a genius. Obviously not new news, but still. Freakin' genius.

'Wow, you've changed your tune!' said Sasha. 'A few weeks ago, Wales was too far away, now you're casually suggesting we all pop across to Paris.'

Hetal threw a cushion at her in reply, then pulled out her phone, no doubt to find out the cost of tickets. But what about Nell? I looked across at her. She was smiling but I was pretty sure it was fake.

'There's no way you can let her miss this chance,' said Nell.

'Let's do it!' Sasha said.

'Hang on.' Hetal stared at her phone. 'I'm looking at prices. It'll be easiest if we used one card to pay for everything.'

My heart dropped. It would cost quite a bit for us all to go.

'It looks pretty expensive.'

'I've got a bit saved from my job,' I said.

Sasha smiled. 'And I hardly spent any of the money Mum gave me for Switzerland.'

'And I've got my first pay packet. You can have what's left after I've paid Cam back what I owe her,' said Nell.

I frowned. 'Aren't you coming, Nell?'

She faltered. 'No. I can't. But I definitely think you all should. And I'll help plan it. You've got to. For Mrs M.'

Hetal leaned over and gave her a hug. 'Are you sure? It won't be the same without you.'

'Rubbish.' Nell moved away from Hetal. 'Now let's get planning.' We all knew she was deflecting.

Hetal went back to scrolling, every now and then murmuring, 'that's interesting,' and 'the coach is cheaper,' and jotting things down on a scrap of paper.

'What do you think?' asked Sasha.

Hetal looked up. 'I think,' she said, chewing her lip as she added up some figures on the paper, 'it's *just* possible. If we get railcards, and Mum's still got her mad stash of supermarket points. Come on, let's talk to my parents.'

We ran down the stairs in a flurry of dressing gowns and slippers and crowded into the lounge where Hetal's parents were watching TV.

'Good evening, girls,' said Hetal's mum.

'Mum, Dad, we have an idea. We want to take Nani to Paris to see her friend.'

'Elsie's in Paris?' said Hetal's dad.

'Yes. She's seeing her son.'

'And you want my help with paying for it, I suppose?'

'We'll pay you back, we just need to use your card.'

'You girls are so thoughtful,' said Hetal's mum. 'And Nani would love that. She's been so down since she heard about Elsie. I think it's a wonderful idea. But it will be very expensive. When are you planning to go?'

Hetal checked on her phone. 'In a few days' time. Elsie isn't in Paris for long. You don't still happen to be collecting points do you?'

Her mum nodded. 'Been saving them for years. Never quite figured out how to spend them.'

'Well, we might need some, or rather, a lot of them,' said Hetal.

'Sounds like it's all sorted then,' said Hetal's dad, chuckling. He pulled his wallet out of his pocket and handed over a card. 'Just don't go crazy. Let me look at the prices you've got.' He pulled his glasses out and perched them on his nose. 'My word, Hetal, you've found some good prices. I'm going to get you to organise all my travel arrangements from now on.' He chuckled. 'Just don't forget to pay me back!'

'Of course,' said Sasha, as Hetal hugged them both.

We ran back upstairs. We still had to check with our parents, email Elsie, book tickets and plan where to stay – there would be even less sleep happening than usual at this sleepover.

The only niggle was that we'd be going to Paris without Nell – and that felt like a pop song without a beat.

CHAPTER 31
SASHA

I met up with Cam down the road from Hetal's house and walked with her the last bit. My suitcase was rumbling loudly along the pavement and my whole body was twitching with excitement. I love anything like this, surprise parties, unexpected trips. Fingers crossed Hetal's nani would like it too.

Cam rang the bell and we waited, grinning nervously on the step.

We heard Mrs M walking to the door.

'Good morning, girls!' She smiled when she opened the door. 'You're both up rather early, aren't you?'

'Mrs M,' Cam said, looking all flustered. 'We've got a plan and you can't say no.'

'Because you helped us with your great advice,' I added.

Hetal appeared behind her nani, grinning. 'And now it's our turn to make sure you don't have regrets.'

'That's right,' said Cam. 'Because no one wants those.'

Mrs M looked a bit bewildered. 'What are you talking about?'

'Paris,' said Hetal.

She shook her head. 'It's too much for me to manage. I couldn't.'

'But we're coming too. We'll help,' said Cam.

She looked around at us standing in front of her. 'You'd do that for me?'

'Absolutely,' I smiled.

'Definitely,' Cam agreed.

Hetal was nodding. 'Say yes, Nani, please. Just imagine seeing Elsie again.'

Hetal's nani was very still for a moment, then nodded. 'OK, you're on. But we've got lots to arrange – she's only in Paris until next week.'

'There's nothing to arrange, Nani, we've done it already,' Hetal laughed. 'All you have to do is pack a bag. We're leaving in an hour.'

Mrs M gave a little shriek, and flung her arms

around Hetal. Then she held her arms wider and pulled me and Cam in too. Reckon she liked the Paris plan.

Hetal was busy looking through her colour-coded files and giving instructions to her dad. He was replying that he'd lived all his life, all fifty years of it, in the South Hams, and that he knew his way to the coach station. I grinned as Hetal shrugged and checked her map against the signposts.

Cam and I were chatting about which bits of Paris we wanted to see and Mrs M smiled non-stop. It was still early when Hetal's dad pulled into the coach station and stopped. We jumped out and went to get our bags from the boot.

'Now, has everyone got their passport?' Hetal's dad asked, but Hetal cut him off.

'It's all fine, Dad. Everything's under control. OK, this way,' called Hetal, flapping her folders at us.

'When did you get so bossy?' Cam demanded.

Hetal looked at her over her glasses. 'Quiet in the ranks,' she said. 'I'm the trip guide. I have the schedule. I am The Boss.'

'Give a girl a folder, and she thinks she's in charge,' joked Cam.

'If you feel you could do this better?' Hetal offered her the folder, eyes twinkling.

'Not a freakin' chance!' laughed Cam. 'We'd be lost before we started.'

'Hetal, honey, I think you're doing a fantastic job,' said Mrs M, who was looking stunning in her bright sari.

'Thanks, Nani,' Hetal said, grinning at us both. 'Right, let's check we've got everything out of the car, and don't forget to thank the driver.' She gave her dad a wicked grin and hugged him. 'Thanks Dad.'

I caught him saying, 'No, thank you, I've not seen Nani look this happy in months. Now go safe and have fun.'

Cam and I chorused our thanks and we trundled off to find the coach that would take us to London.

CHAPTER 32
NELL

I'd woken early. I rolled over to check the time. The others would be on the coach by now. Just. If they'd made it in time. But, of course, they would have: Hetal was in charge. My heart twinged a bit. Part of me wanted to be with them, but the rest of me knew it would be too much. I wasn't up to it yet.

I was halfway through my second piece of toast, catching up on my messages from the girls, when Mum appeared in the kitchen, yawning.

'Morning, gorgeous,' she said as she kissed the top of my head. 'How did you sleep?'

A month ago, I'd have felt defensive that Mum was checking up on me, monitoring my sleep, like a nurse would, but now things had changed. I'm not exactly sure when, or whether it was me who had changed or her, but it felt … better.

'Alright,' I said, spreading marmalade on a corner and taking a bite. 'But I woke up early.'

'Something on your mind?' Mum flicked the kettle on.

'Not really.'

'Anything you want to share?' Mum asked as she fished a clean mug from the dishwasher and spooned coffee into it.

'It's nothing really. You know that "no regrets" thing I was talking about in yesterday's session?'

Mum nodded. 'I thought that was a really great idea.'

'Well, Hetal, Cam and Sasha are taking Hetal's nani to Paris today, to see her friend who is dying. And I was thinking about them. That's all.'

Mum was quiet as she poured hot water and milk into her cup. She inhaled the steam and took a sip.

'And ... didn't you want to go?'

I thought a moment. Had I wanted to go? 'I'm not sure. I mean, yes, I'd love to, but like this? I didn't think it was...' I searched for the right word. 'Sensible.'

Mum frowned. 'What time's their train?'

'It's not until late this afternoon, but it's from St Pancras. Why?'

'I'm presuming everyone's allowed to have a no-regrets summer?' She was starting to smile.

I nodded. 'I guess.'

'OK, so there's one regret I don't want. I don't want to stop you having the opportunity of going to Paris with your friends. And after all the therapist did say to let you do something outside my comfort zone, just to prove to us both that it's okay. And there's no time like the present. So … how about it?'

My brain stuttered. What? 'But how is there even time?'

'You pack, I'll get dressed and I'll drive.'

'What? All the way to London – that's miles. And it will be so expensive.' A laugh bubbled up. 'Are you mad?'

Mum was suddenly serious. 'If you feel up for going, I'm up for helping you get there.'

I looked into her eyes. They were shining.

'I'm up for it.' I said. 'I'll go pack.' I started to head for the door but stopped and came back and gave Mum a hug. 'Thank you.'

'No problem,' she whispered into my hair.

As I ran up the stairs, I called back. 'I thought you didn't like my friends.'

I heard her laugh. 'I'm still not sure that pink's a good colour for hair.'

I laughed too as I stuffed tops and jeans into a bag. I was going to Paris!

I rang Hetal from the car as Mum twisted her way along the lanes to get to the main road. I felt sorry for the other people on their coach – the squeals and whoops when Hetal told the others were deafening! Then I set about booking tickets, having got all the details and more from Hetal in a very lengthy text.

It took hours to get to London, but I couldn't sleep, I was so excited. I kept checking my passport to make sure I hadn't lost it.

We got to the station with only a few minutes to spare. Mum circled, looking for a spot to park. There was nowhere.

'Look, you're going to have to jump out and go find them,' said Mum. 'Give me a ring when you're on the train.'

'OK,' I said. I could feel my heart rate going up. I tried to remember what the therapist had said about breathing, and how this feeling was nearly the same for nerves and excitement. I'm excited, I kept telling myself, not nervous.

'And Nell,' called Mum as I got out. 'Have an amazing time.' I could tell she was worried, I'd spent too much time looking for her worry lines not to see it, but she was smiling. I leaned across from the passenger seat and gave her a big hug.

'Thanks, Mum.'

Once in the terminal, I started looking for the others. There were people everywhere! There must be more people in this train station than in the whole of Devon put together. How on earth was I going to find them?

'Over here!' Sasha's voice, like a mighty foghorn, sounded across the concourse. I looked around and spotted them in the distance. I waved and ran towards them, dragging my bag behind me.

Sasha got to me first. She bear-hugged me and as she did, I felt Cam, then Hetal, join in. It felt good, like this was where I was meant to be.

'I'm so pleased you're here,' said Sasha. 'I couldn't believe it when you rang.'

'It wouldn't have been the same without you,' said Hetal.

Cam was grinning. 'Yeah, good call.'

I smiled. 'Thanks. And for all your texts. They were, well, lovely.'

We linked arms and walked back towards their bags and Mrs M.

'Ah, Nell, so very good to see you,' said Mrs M. 'Now everyone is here, shall we catch our train?'

'Good plan,' said Hetal. 'I'm pretty sure it's platform 12.' She checked the departure boards. 'Yep, platform 12.'

How did she do that? She has an epic memory.

We pulled and lifted and pushed our bags across the station to the right platform. The train was already there, waiting to leave. We stowed our bags in the luggage area and walked into the carriage. It was clean, well-lit and gave me a buzz of excitement. I really was on the way to Paris.

'Bagsy the window,' said Cam, plonking herself down. A businessman in a suit looked up and frowned at us. This wasn't the quiet carriage, was it?

'Who's got a train picnic?' Hetal asked.

'I've got some food,' I said pulling out bag after bag of snacks and drinks. 'Mum insisted I brought plenty. I think she's worried I won't like the food in Paris!'

'How about you come and sit by me,' said Cam, grinning.

We all laughed.

As the train pulled out of the station, I rang Mum.

'What made you change your mind?' Sasha

asked me when we'd all settled down. 'I mean, you don't have to answer that, if you don't want to.'

I smiled. Cam and Hetal were listening, too, while Mrs M ordered tea from the steward.

'Well, it was Mum really. When I mentioned what was happening today, she said she didn't want the regret of me missing out, and I realised I didn't either. And that was that.'

'And how are you feeling?' Cam asked.

I thought for a moment. 'Excited, a bit nervous maybe, but it feels really good to be here.'

We munched and chatted and laughed as the train sped us towards Paris. The tunnel bit was weird. It was odd thinking that we were under the seabed with all that water above us. In less than three hours we were pulling into Gare du Nord. The air was noticeably warmer, and I decided to take off my long-sleeved top.

'You look lovely without those long sleeves, you know,' Mrs M said softly.

'Thanks.' I smiled at her. She smiled back and nodded.

We weren't meeting up with Elsie till the following day, so once we'd found our hotel, dumped our bags in our rooms and had a freshen-up, we explored the streets near where we were staying. Every corner seemed to have a café with little tables spilling out, where people sat chatting and drinking. Somewhere someone was playing an accordion. As we rounded a corner, there, right in front of us, was the Eiffel Tower. It was stunning.

'I've heard so much about it in French lessons that it feels kind of strange to see it for real,' said Sasha. 'Come in closer everyone, selfie time.'

We walked a bit further before finding a restaurant with checked tablecloths and a menu that suited all of us.

The waiter came and poured our drinks. He was trying to catch Sasha's eye but either she hadn't noticed or she didn't want to.

'A toast,' said Nani, lifting her glass.

'To the four of you and to living without regrets!'

'No regrets!' we said as we all chinked glasses and laughed.

EPILOGUE
NELL

We're sat on a bench: Sasha, Hetal, Cam and me. It's not our bench back home, it's a new one. One overlooking the square in front of Notre-Dame. It only just fits all of us, but we don't care. We're all watching the same thing. Mrs M and Elsie. And we're all a bit choked, to be honest. They're hugging. They've been hugging for a while now. But then I guess they've got some catching up to do.

'Oh, that's so great,' says Sasha, sniffing.

I nod, not trusting myself to speak.

Towering above the square is the massive cathedral with its famous gargoyles and ornate architecture. You couldn't get a more impressive setting. Yet it is the small things in this square that are important today. Friends who haven't seen each other for over fifty years, who are catching up one last time.

'What do you think we're going to be like in fifty years?' Cam wonders.

'I bet you'll still have pink hair,' says Hetal.

Cam laughs. 'Bet you'll all have blue rinses.'

'Will we still be friends?' asks Sasha.

'Of course,' says Cam.

'But people change, lives move on,' Hetal worries. 'How can you be so sure?'

'But that doesn't stop a friendship,' I say. 'Look at those two. One moved to the other side of the world – that was fifty years ago and they're still best friends.'

We watch as the two older women laugh together, both talking at once. It's funny watching them. It's like they're young people only in older bodies and, if I squint, I can see a hint of what they were like when they were young, when they were our age.

'We'll always be friends,' says Cam. 'Friends forever and no regrets.'

ACKNOWLEDGEMENTS

They say it takes a village to raise a child and I reckon it's similar with writing a book.

Firstly to my agent, Hannah Sheppard, for offering wise insights, killer edits and answering my many 'I've got a question…' emails. Your unwavering faith in me has been humbling. Thank you.

Thanks to the amazing Firefly team: my editor Janet Thomas for spotting things I hoped no one would notice, Meg Farr for being totally on it with publicity and Penny Thomas and Rebecca Lloyd for copy edits, fresh eyes and boundless enthusiasm. You are doing great things at Firefly Press and it's a privilege to be a part of it.

To all the writing groups I'm a member of – SCBWI, Ashby Writer's Club and The Vinery Writers – I love sharing our writing journeys.

To Zoe Cookson and Tizzie Frankish; your understanding and support continue to mean everything to me. I couldn't have done this without you. To my friend Abby and my sister Chloe for reading early drafts and reassuring me I wasn't deluded. To the fabulous Mrs C for reading the first thing I ever wrote and then for cheering me on ever since.

To the Doomies – you guys rock. In every way. Thank you.

To Perdita Cargill, Sue Wallman, Jules Bryant, Natalie Flynn, Debra Bertulis, Jo Clarke, Julie Pike, Az Dassu and Lesley Parr - your understanding, support and belief have carried me through.

To the Harbour Bookshop in Kingsbridge for being so wonderfully welcoming to me and my family, way before you knew I was a writer. You are part of the reason I chose to set my story there.

To my mum and dad and all my wonderful family and friends who take the time to ask how it's going; those little comments are like shining gems. But more than anyone, thank you to my husband Mark and my children. Your support and understanding made this possible.

And finally, thanks to you, my reader. You have fulfilled my dream – to have my story read.

Dear reader

If you're not quite ready to leave Hetal, Sasha, Cam and Nell behind, check out my website for extras – there's even a quiz to tell you which one of the girls you're most like, and you can sign up for the newsletter to stay up to date with SONR news. You can follow me on Instagram (kate.mallinder) or Twitter (@KateMallinder) and if you've enjoyed *Summer of No Regrets*, I would love to hear from you, or even better, tell someone else how much you enjoyed it!

#NoRegrets

KateMallinder.co.uk

Kate Mallinder

Kate Mallinder lives with her husband, four children and two cats near Ashby-de-la-Zouch in Leicestershire. She grew up in Solihull and went to college in Leeds. She wrote this book as part of her own 'no regrets' pledge, along with trying to surf, which didn't go so well. If left to her own devices, she'd live on a window seat with a good book and a never-ending cup of tea. *Summer of No Regrets* is her first book.